CAN'T COOK
A LOVE STORY

CAN'T COOK
A LOVE STORY
.....*STILL I AM CHEF*

Amit Tiwary

Srishti
PUBLISHERS & DISTRIBUTORS

Srishti Publishers & Distributors
N-16, C. R. Park
New Delhi 110 019
srishtipublishers@gmail.com

First published by
Srishti Publishers & Distributors in 2012

All characters in this book are fictitous, and any resemblance to real persons, living or dead, is coincidental.

Typeset by EGP at Srishti

ACKNOWLEDGEMENT

The book in your hand is an embodiment of inputs from many people who knowingly or unknowingly helped to create this story.

To acknowledge them all, I must not forget to thank God for making me capable enough, that I am writing this acknowledgement.

I would like to first thank Maa, Baba, uncles, aunts, cousins who inspired me that I am capable of doing bigger things.

This story would not have been a book if Ashish, Sudip and Kaustav would not have been there. Thanks for listening to the manuscript on a regular basis; for making that small cup of lemon tea at night and for adjusting with Khichdi on my cooking schedules. I still remember you all saying- 'Baba bas thoda aur baki hai…' when I was still on the 11th page.

My thanks to Runa (Amrita), Paresh, Betu dada (Bishwajit), Antara Bhabhi, Buni Didi(Leena), Santosh Jeejaji, Archita, Riya, Arpan, Ankur, Ankit, Arnab, Debarati, Debojyoti and Debanjan for being cordial and showing strong bondage since childhood days.

I would like to thank Vikas Jaiswal and Ajay Nikam for their inputs in designing the cover page. Khushboo, Manu, Shraddha,

Sandeep, Archana, Pooja, Shazia & Sonal, I will always remember the joy and ecstasy in your face as the book cleared one hurdle from another.

The team at Srishti can't be forgotten to be praised as they showed faith in me and in my writing.

All those persons in this world who share their names with the characters of this book I owe you all a lot. You gave me the power to imagine.

Special thanks to Shri Amitabh Bachchan Ji. I always thrive to imbibe your values and qualities that gave me the strength to write this book.

Last, but not the least, Shailaja, who during each dismal moment of my life kept me with the trust that it was temporary.

All these would have been in vain if you, my readers would not have spent your time and money for this book. Thank you all for your support.

DEDICATED TO

My Dida- Smt. Prokriti Tewary

Hotel Management...Not only a course but a lifestyle

Dhanbad....My village...My Town...My City

PROLOGUE

*I*t was a customary announcement from the cabin crew on board AI-191 of the 777-300 ER aircraft of AIR INDIA, from CHHATRAPATI SHIVAJI international airport, Mumbai to Frankfurt.

'AIR INDIA TAKES GREAT PLEASURE IN WISHING ALL PASSENGERS A HAPPY DEEPAWALI. WE ARE NOW READY FOR DEPARTURE AND YOU ARE REQUIRED TO SWITCH OFF YOUR MOBILE PHONE.............' I completed my fake concern for the passengers of the flight as I went ahead for the service of sandwiches to all the 88 passengers allotted to me.

Life had been appalling there in AIR INDIA, with the aviation sector in India and around the world facing a big turmoil. The job over the years had been boring and there was nothing new to see around the world. The Eiffel Tower now seemed to be like yet another electricity tower of the city and London Bridge held nothing new.

What would a hawker daily selling Bananas on the Howrah Bridge find anything new there?

Yes of course every time I visited any damn place, there were certainly new things to buy, but thanks to the management of AIR INDIA, they did their best to cut our pockets short.

'Madam, Sandwiches. Would you prefer Veg or non-veg?' I asked to a lady passenger in the economy class as I drew the trolley from the galley through the aisles.

'Non Veg'

'Sure', I said as I handed her serve of food.

'Can you please get me some decaffeinated lemon Iced Tea along with that.' The lady said removing her designer sunglasses as she raised her curvy eyebrows.

I was more stunned with the need of the sun glasses inside the cabin rather than the bizarre customized order placed.

'Sorry Ma'am, can you please come again?' I said. 'Was that lemon…'

'The services in AIR INDIA have degraded drastically' She commented in the ears of the fellow passenger.

I had no other choice than to digest the insult and move ahead. Ahead, to find yet another order like a cup of cappuccino without froth.

I seriously feel like to de motivate the people who try their level best to educate these idiots. They really pose danger to the servers.

All of us like Sanjeevika, Aaditya, Mansi and Namita were the victim. Yes they were also working with me as Cabin Crews and Air Hostesses with AIR INDIA.

The end of the first service propelled everybody to gather at the rear galley.

'We are screwed working here. Nobody damns about our credentials and abilities. Cant things change for us?'Shrugged Adi.

'But why are you taking things seriously? It's a part of our job now.' Sanjeevika exclaimed.

'No yaar. Things are going against me. It's enough. I had a dream but I could not make it through. I don't understand where I am heading towards?' His eyes became soft as he said so removing the mock caviar from the tin.

'You never know what is in store for you. Just do your job, chase them as long as you can.' I said as I appeared like some Gurudev in front of them.

'It is easier said than done.' He slashed.

'Interlink your dreams and you will see that your dreams are never dead.' I quoted as I found everybody getting deep into my words.

'But how are you so confident about your thinking?' Namita asked her first question of the session.

I smiled closing my eyes. 'Because I had seen that happen.'

'What has happened?' the Purser questioned everybody as he arrived.

'Just some usual company whereabouts. We will also enjoy some inputs from you Sir.' I said rotating the subject.

The potbelly of the purser had more power to disintegrate the crowd rather than his speech to integrate them. Soon everyone was again found doing *mise-en-place* (preparations) for the next service.

The flight landed safely with all the customary announcements and we also leaped to collect our luggage and boarded the cab for the hotel. Adi, however was seen lost and inquisitive simultaneously. Perhaps he was moved by my lectures. I was a good motivator.

A smile was generated inside me as I could foresee yet another career in case the AIR INDIA shows me a pink slip. Right, to be a Sadhu, up there in the mountains of Himalaya. But quickly I too realized that whatever I spoke was not a joke and was very much a true fact.

'Sudip.' Aaditya called.

'What was that which you said that you have seen?' he was curious.

My strained eyes looked for a sleep as I said 'I WILL SHARE EVERYTHING AFTER A NAP IN THE HOTEL'

BHUBANESWAR

*T*hey were two of them........ There.............. Together.........
seeking admission after cracking the entrance examination.
 Both tall and athletic. One was specs clad, the other with a
comparatively sharper look. They were calling each other by
names, Aniruddha and Kaustav.

Aniruddha looked a little matured, whereas Kaustav was
delighted at everything he was seeing there.

'O Shit Not Again'! Aniruddha murmured. His eye balls
were fixed at the 'declaration form' at the Institute of Hotel
Management & Catering Technology, Bhubaneswar. His
exclamation continued to a silence for few seconds and then he
said to Kaustav, 'I need to declare that I am free from all of the
diseases listed.' The tone gradually fainted.

'So what? You are perfect.' Kaustav reacted casually.

'It also states Epilepsy'. A sad voice from Aniruddha somehow
reached Kaustav.

Thinking for a while, he snatched the papers from Aniruddha's
hand and filled it. 'Sign it and deposit. They are not gonna do
medicals.'

Payments and other formalities followed and finally both of
them got themselves enrolled at I H M Bhubaneswar.

Splitting the swarm of innocent freshers and their ignorant parents, the duo came out to the nearby restaurants. It had a big Cola signage with small letters reading MANOJ RESTAURANT, though it was technically wrong calling it a restaurant, particularly if it caters to Hotel Management students, that too in front of a catering college.

It was more crowded than a fair price shop. Students were seen in uniforms, gnawing at parathas or omelets and almost every delicacy required by the students. Packets of cigarettes were no exception.

As they moved inside the shade created with scrapped tins and bamboo enveloped with palm tree foliages, they were trapped by a bunch of seniors.

'First Years', one of them screamed.

They both turned in unison, with the luggage applying friction to their movements.

'Yes'. Aniruddha nodded in nervousness.

'*Sir kaun bolega, Tumhara Baap*? The same person shouted with smoke rings around, inviting some attention.

A dark complexioned young man with a broad moustache intervened with a plate of omelet in his hand. His movement in that place guided them that he was the owner of that place, may be Manoj.

'*Jaane do yaar*, they will learn the etiquettes' Manoj said. 'He is your senior'. He turned and continued. Perhaps he tried to increase his customer pool without losing the present.

'We are sorry sir' Kaustav said and Aniruddha repeated. 'Actually we are looking for a good accommodation as we could not get one in the hostel.' Kaustav continued as a naïve giving an idiotic look. He was quite good in disguising people.

'Manoj will help you out.' He said and left allowing them to take a seat to have some food.

Carrying their luggage, they followed a side-kick of Manoj to the address briefed. After walking down for five minutes along the lanes of V S S Nagar Colony, they reached the building- Plot no. 25.

The house owner had got the entire ground floor of this building cleaned and distempered, may be to convince potential tenants with his rates. Eleven beds were arranged in four rooms. The rooms were in fact more congested than the sleeper coach of Indian Railways. Thanks to the windows each room had, that it gave reason to stay there. The house owner, a short man could arrange only one tenant by that time.

There are few species or rather class of people, like Principals, Girlfriend's Father and House owners who are generally viewed as descendants of Hitler. He was no exception.

The two strings hanging down of his otherwise elastic pyjama were speaking aloud of his confused persona. This, Bank of India personnel was perhaps on leave to fix yet another source of income. Renting rooms, oops beds rather.

Without much of a negotiation the duo settled in that place at the rate of Rs Seven Hundreds per month per bed.

'I will brief you about the rules once all these beds are occupied.' He said and left with Rupees two thousands as advance. His Oriya accented Hindi was quite similar to the Oriya script; Confusing and vicious.

'Don't you think it's expensive?' Aniruddha asked as both of them tried settling down in the smallest room of the house. Happy though, not to share the room with anybody else. Nothing than a broad window towards the road justified the rent, at least not sharing the bathroom and commode with ten more asses.

Kaustav was evidently found excited to whatever came on his way. He had plans for his college, new friends and everything though a little scare of ragging haunted him as well. He was there right after his plus two. It was easy to read him. Aniruddha was contrary. When Kaustav was happy hunting, Aniruddha looked as if he was used to the little silences of the life.

I could read these all just because I had also managed a room just opposite to them at GL-36. Quite happy to get it alone.

In no time Kaustav was friends with the already present *Chinki* Guy in the house. 'Binayak' He introduced himself to Kaustav with a pride. 'My father is chief Security Officer to President of India.' He added with arrogance.

The high rental did not offer much resistance to get through an hundred percent occupancy. In a couple of hours the barren house was on fire with eleven different souls from various provinces of India.

Anxiety, excitement and fear enveloped all of them. I also joined them making the count to twelve. Some were happy because of their accomplishments to get into Hotel Management, others dreaming being Chefs of Hotels like Taj & Oberois. I was also one of them but it was tough to categorize Aniruddha. His presence there was also linked with a dream, but it was not vocational. The short conversations were not sufficient enough to get more out of him.

Topic of discussion continuously changed directions until we discussed ragging. 'Ragging is not that intense here. I heard it.' Binayak claimed.

'No, I have heard that they might ask us for a nude parade or even to sit nude on a cola bottle.' Replied the other, scaring everybody.

'Shit man. I won't do any such non sense. I would rather complain.' Came yet another voice.

'Remember, we have to bear these fucking seniors only till the Fresher's welcome. Until then we have to entertain the son of the bitches.' I commented.

The coherent laugh introduced strength in us to fight against the terror occupied in our mind.

The heart beat jumped for a while after a knock at the door. 'Seniors', claimed one and everybody took their position. So tensed that no-body bothered to open the door.

The knock intensified and all were happy to see that it was

the house owner. His hair were now dripping more oil than Begun Bhaja (a Bengali dish).

'So, how are you feeling here? His hospitality was enormous, all that he had learnt while dealing with the Hotel Management students earlier. We felt as if we were residing in a deluxe Suite.

He boasted a lot about the room but that did not seem to have interested the boys. Anyways, this tact is better done before selling.

Carrying a diary with him, he noted down the names, address and Phone numbers of all the eleven students. 'This is in case I need to speak to your parents about you all.' He said taking out his spectacle from the elevated nose. His eye balls travelled like a carom striker.

'No alcohols are permitted here and girls are also not allowed. I should receive the rent by 7th of each month. Anyways don't worry about Raging. Your seniors won't come here.' He said it all strictly but his tone appeared comic as he left with his jerky steps.

The entire speech made the boys repent on their decision of choosing this house, barring the last sentence. They wished the landlord to be true there.

Anxiety mounted to peak as the evening progressed. Little scare on everybody's heart was topped up with some home sickness in few of them.

Yet another knock, but the door was spontaneously opened this time. 'Are you freshers?' A nerd looking guy asked what he was sure off.

'All of you are summoned at GM-6 by the seniors, and listen don't skip the order. These seniors are very dangerous.' He added with sync in his trembling feet and tongue. His state advised us that he was also a fresher and was perhaps badly ragged.

The house owner's last sentence was of course true but the truth had a different meaning altogether.

Around ten seniors were waiting for us. The satisfactions in their eyes were visible as they were viewing us like a prey. All of us stood in a queue with eyes pointing towards feet.

'Welome,' said a surd guy, evidently proving out to be a hospitality student. A brief lecture followed which everybody listened but no one intercepted in their brains.

We introduced ourselves and they laughed at all possible unnecessary reasons. May be that gave them the confidence to rag more. We continued doing all possible non-sense to entertain those seniors. The geography of our faces was in control of all of them.

Shrunk faces, trembling feet and dried throat, all came as an embodiment of disrespect against the respect the seniors wanted to gather.

Different tasks were told to be finished in that night itself by various Mr.X, Mr.Y, and Mr Z out there. The biggest of them was to find the names of these seniors with their home towns. They also told us to get or hair scrapped off, beard and moustaches shaved.

'Get rid of all those stuff even from warehouse and not only from showrooms.' I remembered the fucking seniors laughed hysterically saying that.

'Everybody must carry six essentials at any given point of time' was yet another regulation framed. Though I could somewhere relate the first five essentials as per the industry viz Pen, Matchbox, Bottle Opener, Handkerchief and Scribbling Pad; yet I could nowhere create a connect with the sixth essential- 'Condoms!!'

All these had done one thing good. We started getting closer, particularly me with Aniruddha. Not actually he smiled when he was happy or cried when he was sad. What came out of him was very complex and layered.

Our classes started with a boring lecture from the Principal, commonly known as '*Bando Pila*' in the campus. Dark and grey hair plastered on his scalp with a slant forehead bearing wrinkles.

His thick moustaches coiled down near the edges as it tapered, resembling the tail of a chameleon.

The sounds of his Oxford boots suggested as if he had tried to increase the height by an inch with wooden block under the heels.

His hair combed and sliced into two segments as if he needs to put vermillion to prove his marriage.

He started with his primitive theories in the welcome speech in front of the gathering of one hundred and twenty students, with an even ratio of boys and girls. Being the first day, they tried to be focused, but the intensity faded as classes progressed.

Cutting, chopping, mixing, baking roasting, frying were the terms more commonly used by us. Beers, wines, whisky and Rum were not far behind. Students by the end of a month had it in their mind that in which stream they need to excel in their career.

Though Aniruddha was equally good in all the Subjects, he preferred Food Production, aiming to be a chef. Kaustav imitated, though he was not sure. Even I was on the same track.

'I want to cook; to create new foods and to create various concepts of foods. Only then I aim to open a restaurant and..........' He said gradually trying to hide the following sentence.

Six months into the course, life had assumed a pattern, though different for different individual. Girlfriends were the priority of few, and nostalgic studies for others. But the major chunk was crazy about *masti* (fun) *with daru* (liquor) as they described it.

One day into the Food Production class, with around 40 students in different work tables, amidst of chicken joints marinated with chopped garlic and thyme, Kaustav exclaimed as he spoke to someone over his cell phone- the second-hand piece he recently purchased.

His right hand, still holding the marinated drumstick, rose

up to scream and signal. 'Aniruddha; call for you'. He shouted to suppress the echo of cluster of knives making mirepoix (roughly chopped vegetables for stock), and handed over the phone to him.

'Somebody-Jaya', he whispered, coming closer to him & smiled with stitched lips. He was happy for him.

Aniruddha's face was constantly changing emotions between the various words and phrases he uttered between Hello and Bye. At least two pair of eyes was continuously vigilant of this- Mine and Kaustav's.

Giving some extra time for the chicken joints to infuse with the marinade, both of us grilled our brains to reason the same.

'Might be his girlfriend' Kaustav said with his pupil dilated and forehead wrinkled. 'Baba bhi shaana nikla' he said in Hindi, smiling though. We had christened Aniruddha with this name in the recent past.

'But he has never told us about her. Moreover if she is the one, why is she calling after all these days?' I replied.

'Point! Also have you noticed that the way Baba is living? Looks different! I think we need to find it out.' Kaustav spoke exactly what I was willing to.

'Saute'(fry) it properly' the instructor intrudes, pointing towards the sliced onions in the frying pan, preventing us from planning ahead. Our ideas died before realization, suffocated in the coiled hair of his untrimmed moustaches.

Our inquisitiveness grew fast and we chased Aniruddha at all possible times and places. At Manoj's place, he smiled to our questions and laughed at Cafeteria. But he was actually swallowing a bitter pill of distress, coated with the mock happiness.

'Oh Jaya!' He wondered, 'She studied with me for Medical Entrance. She finally got through and hence called.' Aniruddha said.

Six months of acquaintance was sufficient for us to learn that we are being disguised by him. It was later, only with some sentimental and emotional drama that he succumbed to us one afternoon with his past. The past which kept him aloof of everything happening around, at times.

ANIRUDDHA'S DELICACY
(IN HIS WORDS)

3 years back

'*Y*ou never Know, you might get through, or rather you will...' Leena emphasized. 'You are intelligent enough to crack these PMTs.' she added only to boost my moral, which I had lost in this two year of my senior secondary studies.

First a considerably bad result in the exams, clubbed with heinous comparisons around, it appeared as if I reached a dead end. And rightly so, even the local P K Memorial College refused to give me a seat.

I looked around the dust settled on the study materials procured from 'BRILLIANT TUTORIALS.' All that I remembered in those books were the address from where it had been couriered- 'T. NAGAR, CHENNAI.' Baba's face was flashing in front of my eyes. The hard work that he needs put in to cater all these needs of mine was always tougher than reading these books.

'Believe me, they train well. One of my classmate studies there for Engineering. Moreover the fee is also not as high as in Delhi and other cities.' She insisted like a sales person to join a PMT training institute at Bokaro, 40 Kilometers from my house.

'Should I go for it? 'But it will be again an expenditure on me.' 'But if I manage to crack it, the things will change.' 'I will work hard.' There was a short brainstorming within my skull and I finally said- 'I will go.' Leena smiled.

All of a sudden I was seeing myself in a white coat and a stethoscope around my neck.........

....BOKARO STEEL CITY

With two suitcases, one Aristocrat and other VIP and two bags we landed at the 'Naya More Bus Depot' in Bokaro. Among the obvious shouts of the cleaners and vendors we came out of the so called 'THE EXPRESS' bus, which was a misnomer. But all of these were too familiar to me as there were no differences in the standard of the cities were concerned. I had never been to a metro earlier.

I was the only male in the group comprising Leena, my mother and my aunt, Leena being my cousin. Both the mothers were there to get their kids settle in the coaching. Mother's heart or whatever you call it. I was responsible to take the lead.

I leaped towards an Auto rickshaw or 'tempo' as it is called locally.

'Bhai, co operative colony chal raha hai kya?' I asked only to get a negative answer. Similar answers were given by the others as if curfew had been installed in that place. I started heading towards a paanwala to know more about the place only when I realized that the co operative colony was at stone throw distance. As we had some luggage he advised us to take a rickshaw. Though manually pulled, the rickshaw was looking like a newlywed bride with colorful ornamentation.

'Fifteen rupees' the rick puller said.

Ignorant of the fare of that place we nodded and asked him to call for one more rick as we were four in numbers.

I heaved a huge sigh of relief as I entered a road, near which an indicator read Co Operative Colony. I felt relaxed as I was competent enough to carry these women to perfect destination.

The rickshaw passed the main gate and I could see buildings numbered as plots. There were shops of different kinds, not to forget Medineeds and Manpasand.

Suddenly a signage caught my attention. It read 'BOKARO STUDY CIRCLE'.

'There it is' I claimed. Plot No. 50, as the address suggested.

We got down the rickshaw and looked at the coaching centre. It was a 3 storied building and was apparently looking more like a residential complex than an educational institution. A peon came out of the office from the ground floor, and helped us with our luggage.

The office was small with 3-4 persons sitting in that. Names of various students who cracked to the PMTs and JEEs were listed and we hoped seeing our names there soon. We were told about the training programme and the admission

The principal was a descent middle aged man and the coaching was owned by him. He had devoted the ground, first and second floor for the coaching and the third for his home.

The coaching also had accommodation facilities for the out station candidates. We opted for that facility. After going through the accommodation register, the clerk allotted rooms to both of us.

Plot No. 16 to Leena, where the bunch of girls lived and she had to share a room with two others. Plot No. 25 to me where I had to share my room with a guy. Incidentally it was the same guy who suggested us for this coaching, I mean Leena's batch mate in school. He was Siddhartha.

We headed towards the plot no. 16, to keep Leena's luggage first. It was very near to the coaching and the principal had sent the peon to guide us and help us with the luggage. The colony was planned with not so broad roads. In no time we reached the plot no. 16, which was almost 200 meters away on the road perpendicular to the coaching.

On this small way, my mother's eye struck on a PCO. 'Call regularly.' Mother's heart after all. I was away from my family for the first time.

WE MOVED INSIDE PLOT NO 16. IT WAS A BUNGALOW STYLE HOUSE WITH A NICE GARDEN IN THE BEGINNING. THERE LIVED AN OLD RETIRED COUPLE, WHO WERE THE OWNER OF THE SAME. HE HAD FEW OUTHOUSES WHICH HE HAD GIVEN ON RENT.

There were two outhouses and a dispensary where the old uncle used to practice his Homeopathy. Of the two out houses one was big, accommodating six girls and the smaller one for three.

As we moved inside to speak with the owner, he started before we could, as if he knew who we were and what are we there for.

NO FOODS WILL BE SERVED, BOYS ARE NOT ALLOWED, GIRLS NEED TO DECLARE WHERE THEY ARE GOING APART FROM COACHING, AND NO GOING OUT IN NIGHTS...........and the rules continued.

Mothers were pretty satisfied with the rules but my aunt intervened.

'Can you please allow Aniruddha to Leena's room as they are cousins and might require their help and support?'

An instant 'No' was the reply.

After a long debate over this I was granted the permission to go there but only with uncle's permission each time I do so.

Everybody headed towards Leena's room except me as I pretended to be very innocent and going to a girl's room could degrade my rapport on the very first day.

I was feeling exhausted and hence I parked myself along with my luggage under a temporary shadow between the two rooms. Ignorant of what's happening around I kept on gazing continuously to nowhere. Perhaps I had started worrying for the fact that my mother will soon return back and I will be left alone. It never happened with me earlier.

My thought for fear was disturbed as I saw a girl coming out of Leena's room and quickly entering the other room, with a little significance to my existence there. She did it to and fro and hence caught my attention.

She was looking ecstatic as if she has found a lost love or so. Tall, somewhat around five and half feet, with a slim figure, oval face and blunt hair which were oiled profusely, clad in a frock with a floral print.

'What is she doing', I asked myself, dazed by her activities.

'Come inside', said Leena as if everybody remembered me off late that I was standing outside. Or perhaps that girl had reminded them of somebody standing outside.

I went inside with utter shyness as was my nature as far as girls are concerned that too in front of my mother and aunt.

I must give credit to the girls as there were no bra and panties being hung around. They might have removed them with great swiftness. Thanks to them, otherwise I would have been even more perplexed.

'Sit, why are you standing outside' my aunt questioned.

No, actually house owner uncle….

And before I could complete she again said- 'Look, you have to be smart now. You are away from the family and need to look after yourself.' She delivered all the notions that she had for me.

Leena intervened as she introduced me to the other two girls in the room. 'He is my bro- Aniruddha'

She turned towards the girls and so did I. I saw both the girls there. One was a studious looking, specs clad and Leena introduced her as Seema Agarwal from Dhanbad. She gave me an obvious look without uttering anything.

The second girl was a familiar face for me by then. She was the same who was chirping and flickering around, when I was outside.

'And she is Ruchi, my batch mate in school and hence obviously from Dhanbad' claimed Leena. She showered a courtesy smile and so did I. I frankly had the tendency to avoid situations like this as I fail to understand the protocol of these situations.

Also I was scared as she was from same school as Leena's and hence was superior to me. But I somehow gained courage and asked- 'So you knew that Leena was joining this coaching'

'No I had no ideas of this. I was really surprised and happy to see Leena here. Actually I shifted to Carmel School Dhanbad from Digwadih after my ICSE board, so we are meeting after a gap of two years', was her reply and first words to me.

It was too much of knowledge for me but I could understand the happiness and her reason for being ecstatic.

A lot of feminine talks followed simultaneously with arranging the rooms. There were three beds in the room, with one bathroom and one kitchen attached. Though they were getting food from the coaching, still Ruchi had a click gas stove with her, may be for some tea and coffee.

In all these time we were offered tea by Ruchi and I relished on it and so did others. The girls were going to take bath one after another and I dumped my face into one of the biology books owned by Ruchi. 'Dinesh's Biology for pre medical tests' it read.

Soon I noticed Ruchi coming out of the bathroom like morning dew. I could make it out from their conversation that she had done shampooing of her hair and may be a weekly oiling of the hair as noticed earlier. She was looking cute and innocent and I felt like to see her constantly, but could not with my mother, aunt and Leena around.

After completing the settlement there, we moved ahead towards Plot No 25. Both Leena and Ruchi accompanied us. By now I could make it out that it was Ruchi who would be closer to Leena and not Seema.

Just after a single left down the lane we reached plot number 25. We had nothing to discuss with the owner there. We moved inside the outhouse to find Siddhartha there. He was overjoyed seeing me there, though we were meeting for the first time.

'Come in, how are you aunty and' so on.

I felt it more like a drama than realistic.

We got ourselves inside to find out what could be said as the typical way of maintenance by a bachelor guy. There were two beds, though one was pretty fine the other was dumped with books, pillows, bed sheet, stationeries, towels and what not. Thanks, god that there were no under wears around.

It was dark inside the room. He switched on the lights. Everyone managed to sit somewhere and Siddhartha helped me in adjusting with my belongings.

'Let it be like that. We will adjust everything later' suggested Siddhartha.

But I continued with my eyeball constantly rotating towards Ruchi. She was persistently looking at the door, perhaps was lost in a big thought, may be something as big as issues of corruption and terrorism in the country or may be about me. I wondered.

The rotating hands of the wrist watch propelled my mother and aunt to take a leave. We kept everything in same condition and I along with Siddhartha went to the bus depot to see them off. Leena and Ruchi went back to their rooms as we had to go for our coaching classes in the evening.

I felt like crying when my mother was leaving but somehow managed to escape. I was in a new world altogether and it was just the beginning. We reached our room and hurried for the first class of the coaching.

By then, it was 5 pm and Siddhartha and I walked towards the coaching institute. Siddhartha suggested me to call Leena and go together as it was the first day. After thinking for a while, I went inside the plot no 16 and asked uncle if I can call them for classes.

Uncle said 'Yes, but don't make it a habit'.

'Thanks', came out of my mouth but 'SAALA BUDDHA' subdued.

I moved up to their room and knocked. Surprised to see me

there, Ruchi said anxiously- 'Did uncle saw you coming'. She was wearing a long frock or so in yellow and black. I don't know the name of that dress but she was looking stunning.

'Yes I took his permission, but he seems to be little over reactive' I replied.

'Anyways let's move for the classes, we might get late. Also Siddhartha is waiting outside' I added.

I came out with Ruchi and Leena. Seema was in the morning batch. Joining Siddhartha, the four of us reached the coaching.

It was little crowded there all the faces were looking new. Siddhartha guided us for our classroom and then he left for his class. I went inside the class along with Ruchi and Leena. The classroom was half full. We managed to find some vacant seat and sat together.

'*Saala ek saath do do ladki*' a very prominent voice entered my ears. I turned around to see the commentator.

I could not exactly make out the exact origin but I could find the group. They were still staring at us. I wanted to show my heroics but Leena did hold my hand and Ruchi shook her neck in negation.

I was lost somewhere when our professor entered. Mr. Amitabh Roy was there to teach us Physics. Fat as elephant and hair as big as Ruchi's hair, he was least bothered about anything else than physics. His trousers were half down the buttocks when he turned around to write something in the blackboard.

Siddhartha had told me that he was ranked all India second in the IIT JEE, and was studying at IIT Kanpur, but he was thrown out because of some drugs issue.

He started directly with some linear motion in two dimensions. I felt as if I had heard this before, but for me the life was still uni-dimensional and I was thinking when this training will get over. Actually I was missing my home.......my family.......everything.

The first day in Bokaro came to an end. I had a chat with leena at the end of the class. 'Siddhartha is a good guy; he will guide you in all possible ways.' She said.

The next day started with a fresh morning after Siddhartha's alarm clock rang aloud at around 5.00 am. He had a primitive alarm clock whose sound was capable enough to wake up dead bodies in a morgue. To add to the cruelty, he used to put on the alarm and then took out its keys and kept it at any corner of the room. Reason being to get up at any cost.

Siddhartha was good at studies and was a disciplined boy. He introduced me with all the residents of the out houses.

The first to meet was Rana. He was actually a scholar from *Bhagalpur,* a small town in Bihar. He could not appear for his plus two examinations last year due to some medical problems, and hence was there to appear this time. He had a servant with him for his food and all and particularly for tea of which he was very fond of.

A general knowhow of each other and then he offered us some tea. It was really nice, just the way I used to like it. He had a small room but well maintained. I was impressed.

Next to go was *Sharan Bhaiya.* A 'bhumiya*r*' by caste and a Medical Representative by profession. Through his words I could make out that he was not happy with his job and hence was carrying its burden along with his hundred kilos structure. Though a regular drinker, he had a pristine heart, is what I could read out of him.

Later Siddhartha took me to local shops so that I could purchase daily use materials. Siddhartha guided me for the same and we came back with products such as Talcum powder, nail cutter, etc as per his brand choice. I felt as if he had a better understanding in these as wel.

All through the day was passed with little study and more gossip, making it a point that it was the first day and hence we must understand each other better.

We shared talks about our past and families and many other things.

Come evening and we got ourselves ready for the classes. I did not call Leena as I had to speak to that commentator.

Reaching early I could see everybody coming there. Soon I could manage to see a sturdy looking guy coming out of an auto. He was the person I was waiting for.

Seeing his strong built I had no intention to fight with him. Also I could make it out that he was there with a gang. But anyways I had to sort out the issue that occurred last evening. At last, nature speaks out.

I leaped towards him from the back and keeping my left arm over his shoulder I said '*Aur boss kya haal hai*' I smiled.

His eyes suggested that he was not expecting something like that.

'F fine'….. He uttered.

'I am Aniruddha from Dhanbad. It was a good joke yesterday. I liked it. Anyways one is my sister and the other is her friend. I guess you don't date sisters.' I said in a very reserved voice.

It acted fast. Soon he came back with a positive approach and said- 'Sorry yaar, we did not know it was like that.' He paused and continued 'Can we be friends?'

After thinking something, don't know what I said- 'why not, let's start with some samosas', and we moved towards the sweets shop *Manpasand.*

He was Samit Bhattacharya. A guy of somewhat my kind, but with a lesser touch of emotion.

By the time we returned, the class had already begun. Leena and Ruchi were there and they were shocked to see me with Samit that to as cozy as bosom pals.

As the class finished and both Ruchi and Leena came rushing to ask me or rather warn me about whatever they saw.

'Why were you speaking to him?' Leena interrogated.

Ruchi did not say everything, but her eyes insisted that I must not do that.

'You know, he is a nice guy and it was all a matter of confusion yesterday. He apologizes for it now.' I defended.

'Your choice, but I feel you must maintain a distance from him.' Leena suggested as an elderly sister.

I was not much interested in that advice as I had a habit to go by my instincts. Still I nodded my head.

As a silent group we returned to our rooms. I had my dinner and retired to my bed. I arranged my books on the bed near my pillow and tried to concentrate on studies.

This was a transformation in me, most probably because I found Siddhartha studying intensely and so should I. The fact that the procurement of coaching fees was not so easy made me to realize what was expected out of me. Things continued as such for few days.

In the midst of all these there were Tests conducted at the coaching. To my surprise I topped in my batch. Ruchi, Leena.... Everybody had scored less than me. I was happy and now I had an identity in the class. Even girls used to pay heed to my words.

It was almost a week now in the coaching and I felt better after the initial home sickness. I was probably more happy as I was going back home on 27th of Sep for Durga Puja.

Siddhartha, Ruchi and Leena were to accompany me as all were from Dhanbad. I was euphoric as I was going home after a gap of eleven odd days. Most importantly I was going to meet Amit Manu, my batch mate in school; who was also coming from Delhi.

I was more behaving like a newlywed bride, who was returning to her parent's house from in-laws for the first time. As soon as we reached the Bus Stand, I rushed to board the bus without caring about others and occupied the last window seat.

I had no clue of the other three. Perhaps Siddhartha helped the girls to manage somehow.

The journey of one and half hour seemed to be like a day and half. The bus was overcrowded as if it was carrying goats and sheep. Anyways, I managed to get down at *Putki Thana More*.

As soon as I got down I looked for Leena. To my surprise Ruchi also got down. I did not asked anything, instead tried to show that the bus was very crowded and so I could not take care of them.

'You know, the bus was so overcrowded that the conductor could not reach me for fare.' I grinned sheepishly.

'It was because Ruchi paid for your fare' Leena said and posed serious.

'Ruchi?' I repeated the word or rather the name.

'Yes', came with a punch from Leena.

'Thanks, I will pay you back sometimes. Actually I don't have change now' I said to Ruchi, without seeing into her eyes.

'No it's fine. I mean just okay. We are friends after all'. She said quite descriptively.

I did not pay much heed to the meaning of those words but I was happy as I felt I saved twenty rupees or so.

'But where are you going, I mean I heard that you stay at Dhansar, so you could have well got down at Bank More.' I suggested.

'I am coming to your home. Why? Should I not'. She said ignorantly.

'Why not...I mean...Yes....but', were astonishing replies from me. Both the girls started laughing.

'Ruchi's papa has told her that he will pick her from this place as she would be alone waiting there at the next stop.' Leena tried to make me understand.

It meant that we will have to wait until Ruchi's papa comes. I was not actually happy as I wanted to reach home at the earliest.

We waited for around half an hour. No one came.

'You all go, why you both are unnecessary wasting time. My father will come in some time and I will go', Ruchi said in a slow voice.

'No yaar, how can we leave you alone? Either you come with us or we will wait here', replied Leena.

Soon I could see a sigh of relief in her face as I found a man coming out of a Maruti Omni. He was not that old, perhaps late forties, had a strong built and looked strict. He looked through his spectacles which seemed to be prominently fixed in his elevated nose.

As he came closer I could make out that he had a wheatish complexion, and was chewing something constantly, surely not a chewing gum.

Reaching us he spat a stream of brown liquid, like a snake throwing a fine stream of venom, when I realized that he was actually chewing paan.

'Namaste Uncle' Leena and I said in unison.

'Namaste, Thanks for waiting so long, actually my driver did not arrive and I am not good at driving cars' he said in an appealing tone.

'*Lekin aap Scooter se to aa sakte thhe*, they are waiting for so long'. Ruchi rejected her father's petition.

'Sorry and Thank you for waiting' Ruchi said

'For what? After all we are friends' I replied without wasting any time.

She left for her house with her papa and so did we...but in an autorickshaw.

PEEL, CUT AND GRIND

Durga puja was over. We celebrated it in the best possible manner and in the same traditional way I have been doing it for the last 18 years.

The very thought of going back to Bokaro started torturing me. But I had no choice left. It was 3rd of October that we again left for Bokaro.

As we reached my room, I found Siddhartha already present there.

'It was just an hour back that I reached' he said.

The room looked different. The otherwise mute room had made way for melodious tunes of Rafi and Kishore.

Yes, he had brought a music system along with him. I found him very excited about the same.

He played some music in it and I enjoyed it taking a quick nap. Soon I was in deep sleep and woke up only before the coaching classes. I somehow managed to reach in time. Siddhartha bunked his extra classes. Perhaps he was overjoyed with his music system.

It was everybody there. Ruchi, Samit…etc. we chatted a lot and then dispersed as the class begun. By this time Samit had been a common friend of all of us.

The class started with a big bang. The professors were more

active and there was huge pressure to cover up what was being taught, particularly for me. Only I knew how I had wasted my two years. But I had a dream now; I wanted to be a doctor.

I came back and tried to concentrate more on my studies. Sometimes I visited Leena's place, but only if required urgently.

The results in the next test forced me to think that I was not really pushing it hard.

Soon I recognized that I was not able to memorize my Biology lessons as I had stopped reading aloud. I had a habit of memorizing text by reading aloud.

With cups of tea in my hand, I sat with Siddhartha. 'My bio scores are going down yaar. I wonder what should I do?' I said.

Sometimes you end up sharing your problems with the person causing them. Here also it was no different.

Actually I was cautious studying Bio as I usually read it aloud. I did not want to disturb him.

'Can you please suggest me a way out where I can memorize without disturbing you' I asked.

'You better learn the art to memorize in the other way as I won't allow you to disturb me', he spontaneously replied in a blunt way.

I was actually not expecting something like this from him. After all I felt we are getting closer. It did hurt my ego and questioned my stubborn.

Soon I decided to go for reading aloud and memorizing. 'After all I was also paying half the rent of the room.' I thought.

Continuing for a day or two, I felt as if he was not actually getting disturbed.

Leena was the nearest resort to dump any feelings.I conveyed whatever was happening with me.

'He is like that only. I know him since childhood' Ruchi said, handing a cup of tea to me.

'Actually both of our fathers work together and hence we know each other since childhood. We also went to school in the same jeep.' She justified at my astonishment of her knowhow..

I looked composed and did not utter anything.

'What happened, now you are reading aloud, so it's okay na?' she questioned.

'He does not speaks to me directly and I am feeling very lonely' I replied like a kindergarten boy.

'So what, we are here na, speak to us. After all you have the visa to our room as wel. We are good friends'. Ruchi said. I found her more concerned than Leena.

I went back to my room and started studying. Soon Siddhartha joined with a pen and paper, solving some calculus. But he did so along with is music system aloud. I could well understand his motives.

I somehow continued till the evening and went for the classes.

I discussed the matter with Samit. He was a rather callous guy and used to take things as easily as possible.

'*Saale ko utha lete hain*' he shouted.

I was not enjoying these at all. Somehow completing the class I came back to room. There was a pin drop silence in the room, or noise only when I am reading.

I did not want to fight with Siddhartha. I was in a fix.

I again went to Leena's room but was shocked to see the room was divided into compartments by the girls. Here the situation was even bitter.

There was a cat fight between Seema and Ruchi over a similar issue as I had with Siddhartha. Ruchi could not learn until she reads aloud, and this thing hampers Seema's concentration.

I returned without saying anything. Later, I then moved to the coaching and narrated my problem to the principal.

He listened to all like an innocent child, hearing to grandma's stories; and smiled but preferred not to speak anything.

Call him a real supportive gentleman or anything; he quickly came to my rescue.

'You can do one thing, come to my house whenever you feel

like and study there. You will not face any such problems there'.
He said.

'I will also tell my wife about the same.' He added.

I could not believe that he would extend up to that to help
me out. I now had a greater respect for him than earlier.

I quickly rushed to Leena's outhouse to share it all. But to my
surprise none of them were amazed hearing the fact. Instead they
first smiled and then laughed unanimously.

Their laugh dehydrated my self confidence. In fact I felt as
if they were laughing for the fact that I went to the Principal for
this petite issue.

I could regain my lost poise and patience only when Leena
came to my rescue and gave me a detailed view of the story. I was
actually looking at the tip of the iceberg.

'It was Ruchi and me, who went to the principal and gave
him a thorough view of all the problems being faced; right in the
morning. We also told him about similar problems faced by you.'
Leena said clearing the doubts and stopped only to let Ruchi
follow.

'So it was decided that everybody who read aloud can come
to his house.' She said with a cheeky smile on her face.

I could well remember and understand the smile on the
Principal's face by then.

I went back with an attitude to solve all the differences I
had with Siddhartha. I spoke to him about my plans from the
next day. He was also found pretty satisfied with the remedy
suggested.

Evening classes were again ordinary, with the physics
professor teaching about 'LUX'- the unit of light. Few defined
it as the 'Beauty Soap of Film Stars.' Though I was also in the
cluster with Samit, disturbing the class, I was however not caught
unlike others who were thrown out. Probably my rapport saved
me.

THE SPARK IN THE BURNER

*a*new day, with new beginning. I had to go to the princi's house for my studies. It was a little ill at ease, going to someone's house daily for studies, but I had no choice.

I woke up early in the morning, a little earlier than usual. I got myself ready and headed towards the coaching, with a Zoology book and an urge to excel in the PMT anyhow.

I was happy to see my Princi standing outside. As I approached him, he took me to his house and introduced me to his wife. She knew all about it and asked me for a cup of coffee.

Though I wanted to say 'yes', but my shyness came in between and said 'no thanks'. She guided me to their living room but I preferred the terrace than the rooms.

I selected a corner and started with the digestive system of Cockroach. I was lost somewhere in the gizzards of the stingy cockroach, when I found Ruchi there. I could identify with the situation and surroundings that she was also there for the same motive. I to mean studying.

With a smile on her face, she selected another corner, diagonally opposite to mine and started reading aloud. She was also digging out the Cockroach as we had a test in the evening.

Results followed the Tests and I was again the highest scorer. My rapport was maintained or rather enhanced.

Now it was a routine for me to study in the classes, does little fun with Samit after that: and returning to room. In the room I only used to study Physics and Chemistry as Siddhartha used to help me out in any troubles. We were again getting closer.

'Saale, tu to hero ban gaya hai.'

'Why', I replied

'You are always in the discussion among the girls' he quoted

'And how do you know that' I questioned

'Because I am very good in knowing about girls, and what they think' he boasted.

'It's all Bullshit'. I commented. 'Let's go for a tea out' I continued.

'Fine', he approved' and we went out for some tea at the bus stand at around 1.00 am.

Our talks rotated around our career, films, songs, life and what not. Sometimes serious, otherwise filthy. I started feeling comfortable sharing things with Siddhartha. Actually 'Siddhartha' had turned to 'Sid' for me in no time.

Next few days were pretty similar with each other as if everything was very much customized. Morning began with studies in the princi's house sand the night ended with some chat with Sid. Study was given importance but so did other things as wel.

I was in constant touch with Leena as wel as my parents back home which fuelled my will to crack the PMT. As far others were concerned, Seema Agarwal had left the coaching due to some personal issues and was replaced by Jaya Banerjee. She was also from Dhanbad and was Ruchi's friend there. The trio of Leena, Ruchi and Jaya now lived together without differences between them.

Jaya, as a character was a short heighted girl, who was quite friendly and adaptive to situations. She quickly understood the minds of the girls and boys around.

Nevertheless, my timidity and apprehensions for Ruchi were on its last legs (disappearing) as we continued studying together.

Now we used to talk when studying as wel and our seats in the terrace were also not that far off.

'Aniruddha' she called me and gained my attention as we were studying.

'Yes' I replied casually.

'How can you be so good in everything? I mean you study exactly same what I do here, yet to top the examinations; the professors praise you in the class and above all you are friends with everybody in the class' She said with some jealousy in her eyes.

'I wish I could be like you' she continued.

I was dumb hearing that. No one had ever said such praising words for me in the past. That too, from a girl; it was never expected. Without thinking about the realities of her words I started feeling great.

I wanted to hear more of these and who does not. But somehow I controlled myself and said 'it's nothing like that', pretending to be modest.

'You know, Leena always keeps on telling how much you are loved by your relatives and friends. And above all you are so simple'. She said.

I could only reciprocate with a smile but I was feeling little shy as wel.

'You know, you are also very good' I said without giving any description.

She initially kept silent and then smiled looking into my eyes and said-' But there is a problem with you. You are very shy. Isn't it?

I looked nervous but gathered some courage to say a big 'NO'. I shake my head for long.

'See it has been long now that we are studying together here, you also visit our room to meet Leena, yet you hardly speak with me'. She justified.

'Can we be good friends? I can learn a lot from you.' She was excited.

'Yes, why not', was an obvious answer relating to the gravity of the situation.

We were back to studies but I could not concentrate. After a while when I could again focus on the book, she asked me clear her doubts about Gymnosperms and Angiosperms.

I gave a lecture on the subject as she listened to it like an obedient student. I felt that I did my best to satisfy her query.

At around 1.00 pm we left for our respective rooms, but together for the first time. I waved my hands as she came near her gate, and so did she with a smile.

I came back to room and shared everything with Sid.

'Great going, man. I told you na'. He said as he tried to prove himself right.

'But take care. You never know these girls. Even god has failed to understand them' he said quoting the old proverb.

'No..No..Nothing like that from my side: and from her side as wel I feel' I defended.

'Let's see' he ended as we went to sleep.

I was deep engrossed in the Human respiratory system as Ruchi came inside the Terrace with a smile on her face, making it continuity with yesterday's bye.

'Hi, how are you' She said

'Fine, and how about you' I replied.

'Good Yaar'. Words I never heard from a girl for me.

'Actually we were discussing about you yesterday in the room' she said

'What?'I questioned.

'Actually all the girls were bullying Leena that we would flirt with you' she said 'and she was sacred hearing that' she continued

'Obviously she will be. After all she wants me to save from all of you as she is my sister' I replied with a cunning smile.

'Do you think me like that' she asked.

'What?' I responded

'Someone who can harm you.' She said as she became serious.

'I was just kidding....'I said to bring her back to normal. Any ways let's study as we are just not doing what are we here for. She realized and we started but the session was very short lived.

Soon she interrupted the fungal growth which I initiated in the Biology book.

'Can I ask you a silly question?' She said and continued without waiting for me to reply. 'Do you wear jeans?'

'Yes.' I said after thinking a lot about the reason for this query.

'But I have never seen you in them' She pondered as she said so.

'Actually I have not brought any of them to Bokaro' I reasoned.

'Okay, do it next time you go home.' She suggested.

I actually started being diverted from my studies, but to be true to myself I was enjoying chatting and being with her. I could study the innocence in her through the questions she put forward.

'When are you coming to our room next? I am going to show something.' She said

'In the evening probably as there are no classes. But what's that?' I exclaimed as I interrogated.

'See it then only', was her reply.

We practically studied nothing by the time it was 1.30 pm. We left for our rooms together waving hands, which had been a protocol by then.

I reached home, had my lunch and was waiting for the evening. Just after the sun set both me and Sid went to the girl's room.

We had serious chat about our career as we sipped the Tea made by Ruchi along with some cashew nuts which her father had sent only for her.

'Look this is what I wanted you to show'. She said in front of everybody as I found her taking some greetings card out of a packet.

They were of different shapes, size, color and different matter, sent from various sources like friends, cousins, sisters...... and so on.

She took each one out and introduced me with the sender as …. 'Zeba, this is my best friend. We studied together for last 12 years. Now she is in Allahabad.

I was amazed with what was she doing owing to the reason for the same and so were others. But she was frantically detailing each of them. Her hysteria stopped only to show me a card from a guy called Manish. She remained silent as I read through the text in the card. It was tough to conclude about the relation that guy shared with Ruchi from that text.

Thorough silence in the room prevailed until Jaya said- 'Manish is her cousin brother' to my rescue. Though I did not want to show it off, yet everybody could understand that something is being cooked between Ruchi and me.

I somehow managed to come back to normal as I was very scared of Leena, and we left their room.

'I don't know what Leena would be thinking' I asked Sid with some hopes of positive reply.

'I could read from her eyes that she did not like what was happening' he replied

'But that's not my fault. I don't have any intensions of anything as such' I defended

'May be, but I feel that you are getting attracted. And if yes, you must admit, without thinking about anybody. It's your life after all. But remember what I said you about girls….' He said everything together, as if he wanted to be politically correct.

Though things were curling up, still I could feel the urge to meet Ruchi the next day. It was something that I could not lie to myself.

Sometimes I bothered whether Ruchi too was developing some feelings for me or I was being carried away. But who cared. I was in love after all.

HEAT THE FRYING PAN

*M*y apprehensions grew even stronger in the next morning when she asked- 'Aniruddha, do you have a girlfriend', in a low voice.

'No', I said with a low in confidence as she asked me this question.

'Don't hesitate, and I won't mind. I am your friend after all'. She said with a heavy heart.

'But all of a sudden.....what happened?' I asked shockingly.

'No, actually I thought we were good friends by now and you will not hide any of your secrets from me. Sorry that I expected quite a lot.' She said slow loaded with sentiments.

I was still guessing as she continued- 'Who is Jyotsna'?

I felt from the blue as I heard the name. 'How did she come to know about her', I asked myself as I pondered that no one in Bokaro could relate me with her.

She replied as if she heard the voice within me, 'Sorry, but I had read a letter and seen a photograph sent to you by someone called Amit Manu. The peon gave it to me to pass it on to you but.....I could know about Jyotsna from that letter only. You have posed nicely with her.' She completed slowly.

A huge laughter by me broke the silence and the gravity established in the atmosphere. I continued laughing and ended up in a cheeky smile but she looked lost.

'Manu is my best friend and it is his regular habit to tie me with someone or another. Anyways where is the letter?' I asked.

My words came as a relief, which was pretty clear on her face. At least I could read that as she took the letter out of her book and handed over to me.

'It's entirely your fault. You only did not brief me about your friends and past.' She complained as I completed the letter with a smile.

'Okay I will *meri maa*', I agreed.

I was looking happy remembering Manu's letter. I looked into her eyes and then rolled my eyes over my stomach and said 'let's go for some *samosas*, I am really getting hungry'.

She smiled and started walking, thereby endorsing my idea. I followed her up to *Manpasand*. We ordered for some *Samosas* and coke, got them packed, and moved back to the terrace.

As I relished the snack, Ruchi threw scores of question to me related to me, my likes, dislikes, parents, and friends and so on. I kept on answering them as if appearing for a viva- voce. She also provided inputs about her.

I had to remember many things after that, viz- She loves Chicken, Chocolates & Ice Cream, her birthday, her hometown and that she throws her milk in the wash basin each time her mother offers her.... and many more things.

'Girls perhaps intend to show their love for chocolates and ice creams, just to prove their feminism.' I felt. I had also read somewhere that chocolate was aphrodisiac. But I had no intentions to investigate.

I was engrossed in something called love, without any declaration. I was quite visible that both of us were happy at each other's companionship. Time moved, and so did everything.

It was almost three months in Bokaro by then. Many a times my parents and uncles came to visit me. It kept me in the hunt for a seat in the medical college. Every time somebody comes to meet me, I made it a point to take them to Leena's place. Hence

Ruchi was now well acquainted with my family, and so were they. Actually my father was very impressed by the Tea she used to make.

I was also a known name in her house by then but just because of my good results.

I used to discuss the status of the relation I was sharing with Ruchi, but Sid pretended to be somebody who plays safe.

Soon came Siddhartha's Birthday. It was on 22nd of December.

I along with Ruchi, Leena, Jaya and Sid were a group by then. Samit also sometimes peeped into it, otherwise was related to me only.

A very good gift was suggested to be presented to Sid, the idea did not materialize as Leena and Jaya had already purchased their gifts.

'Let only both of us gift something to Bhai Jaan' she suggested.

She had started calling Sid with that name. Maybe she wanted to portray that Sid was his brother and no one else.

'Fine', I said and we moved out.

We roamed about the shops of the vicinity but could not close on what to be purchased. I was getting lethargic but she was still athletic.

'Shopping with females is worse than any other nightmare.' I remembered my father's words, as I followed Ruchi.

Siddhartha came to my rescue, when I found him on the streets going somewhere. I shared with him the trouble as Ruchi was busy in finding something great for Sid.

'I want a Mouth Organ, get me that.' He said bluntly

I proposed the idea to Ruchi and she liked it, without knowing that from where it originated.

We bought a Mouth Organ, and got it packed. Siddhartha joined us from nowhere, giving Ruchi no idea that he was chatting with me few minutes back.

Ruchi hid the gift as soon as she saw Sid.

'Arre yaar, where are you guys roaming around.' Sid asked

'No, just like that, we were feeling little bore and we came out'. I supported the lie.

Without any hint for his Birthday to Ruchi Sid said, 'So what are your plans for the new year?'

'I am actually going to Dhanbad' he added without letting us reply.

Everyone remained silent, lost in their own world. Ruchi spoke to break the silence, 'In fact I am thinking to give someone a greetings card, but wondering if he will receive it or not.' she said in a serious tone as if the matter was a critical as going for a nuclear attack.

'Of course he will receive it. He would be a dog if he does something otherwise' I said confidently, without knowing of whom she was talking about.

'But who's that, let us know' Siddhartha asked sarcastically.

'You know him, but I won't say his name' said Ruchi.

'Some hints', suggested Sid.

'He is from Dhanbad, studying in this coaching.........'

'He is Arindam', Siddhartha claimed sneakily

'Oh no, you know him even better. Actually he is your room partner.' She said slowly as she leaped a step ahead.

My heart beat came to normal, yet I was wondering about the text and the way the card will be addressed to me.

Ruchi ran to her room citing untrue reasons. I looked into Sid's eyes unable to read what it said.

Now I was just waiting for a single thing, which was the card from Ruchi. It was something like being nominated for an award.

The day arrived when she gifted me the card. It was well before the New Year eve. She handed me the card in the evening, in isolation after the classes were over. She did not say anything, nor did me, but our eyes spoke a lot.

I was stupid or perhaps miser enough that I never thought of giving her a card back.

I took the card and went straight to my room and opened it to find it a regular friendship driven New Year card. I was expecting more, but I felt that being a girl she did not wanted to make the first move anything except friendship.

All these things were happening quite clear in front of Leena's eyes. Though she did not like them, yet she never spoke to me over these. She was actually concerned over me being out of focus from studies. However I was unaware about her feelings in this regard.

I was happy with that card only, but it was Sid who motivated me to think ill of Ruchi quoting ill things about her. He showed me the dire consequences of this relation and hence I must cut things off with Ruchi. I obeyed like an *Al Qaeda fidayeen* in front of Sid and tore the card to pieces.

Siddhartha passed this news to the girls so that the matter gets voltage. It was then only that I could smell some conspiracy.

I still wondered for the motive behind this, may be it had its root in Leena's mind to keep me away from Ruchi. So she might have plotted this in association with Sid.

I was nervous and depressed so as to how I would face Ruchi. I did not want to speak to anybody. Late in the night I woke up and tried to mend the tattered card, that were in 32 pieces. I somehow managed to glue them together. May be my emotions had more power of sticking it than the fevicol.

The night passed in unrest, with thoughts in my mind about the outcome of the mistake I had done. I had decided to meet Ruchi and confess my guilt, though I felt that I would not be able to persuade her after all these.

I woke up before the alarm clock rang, got myself ready and moved towards the coaching centre. It was still closed. I was waiting outside for it to open. I had my Zoology book with me and the mended card inside it.

Soon I saw Ruchi coming. She was also earlier than usual. I turned my dead down in dishonor, as if I had done a big crime. She came closer and asked-

'What happened?'

'Why are you here so early?' she continued ignorantly as if nothing happened.

I did not answer. It was totally silent there apart from some sparrows chirping.

The silence broke after sometime when I said 'Sorry', still keeping my head down.

'I don't feel myself suitable enough to be your friend', I added with a temper of sentiments.

A smile, against my thought was something I could see as I moved my face up. I wondered how it happened and was that real?

'Now don't make faces. You tore the card, so what; it was just the piece of paper that is torn and not our friendship.' She said boldly, without letting me confess as she came closer to me standing on the mid road.

'And I can well understand the reason for doing so. I know Bhai Jaan since long. He must have............'she said as I could see the confidence in her.

I was happy that she knew the truth without my speech. We were so lost in the discussion that a long horn of a car made us realize that the coaching gate was open. We hurriedly went inside as the chauffeur shouted *'marna hai kya....kahan kahan se aa jaate hain.'*

We laughed together and went up the stairs. I showed her the card in the same condition. She was bowled over by the hard work offered, to bring it in that state, though not the original. It also gave her some energy as she hold my hand and said,

'After all these do you still need to say sorry?' She looked into my eyes.

I smiled in reply.

'I am not going to give it back. Now it is a gift to me' she said as she seized it and felt elated.

Things were again back to normal, but I felt that we were now sharing more electrons in the bonding.

Siddhartha went to Dhanbad in the New Year. There evolved a cold war between Leena and Ruchi, though they still pretended to be friends. Jaya was more out of true towards Ruchi than Leena. As far as I was concerned, I was the subject for all above.

THE TADKA

*O*ne thing made way for another. Now Ruchi used to come to our room to study as Siddhartha was not there. We enjoyed each other's company. We shared our lunch and studied together. But our talks were more personal than academicals. In the process of exploring each other better, she whisked each and every aspect of my life. These things however were not known to Leena and others.

In my room she even met Rana, Sharan Bhaiya and also our maid. She advocated as to whom should I mingle with and whom not. Our maid started calling her 'Heroine', due to her looks and she enjoyed it.

Taking an idea out of this I started to flirt.

'You know your chin looks very cute', I said without any previous experience of flirting.

She smiled, educating me of my ignorance.

'I know', She said. I am feeling to have some chocolate pastries. I could sense an opportunity and ran out without uttering anything.

I returned back in some time with two chocolate pastries from a little far away kiosk. I was breathless as I entered the room yet I felt happy for my achievements.

'Are you mad?' She said with a wrinkled forehead. 'I was just not serious as I said that'. She completed.

'Yes, I am', I said as I smiled and ended up in laughter. It could well prove my efforts to make her happy. She joined me laughing, throwing few punches at me.

As soon I placed the pastries in a plate, she shoots on to the pastries, like a famine affected child.

She placed a small piece in her mouth and put one in mine. I closed my mouth and licked her forefinger in the process. It was delicious and it had to be when the service was so personalized.

I could read the 'yumm' of the pastry in her eyes, somewhere I was lost into.

She spoke to bring be back from the dreams. 'Don't spend like these on girls'. She advised.

'I generally don't do that. I do it only when my heart sponsors it.' I defended.

'Is that so?' she asked mischievously.

I did not answer, rather tried to change the subject as I was always worried of some negative effects.

'Ruchi, do you think I will get through the medicals? You know, I feel it will have a great impact on my personal life as well.' I asked sentimentally.

'You will be able to persuade your 'to be father in law' by the results, Right?' she asked.

I smiled in agreement.

'But who is this lucky girl?' She questioned only to answer herself.

'Jyotsna' She came out with a pre meditated reply.

I was in a conjecture, whether she was pulling my leg or was innocently asking this grave question.

To interpret what her feelings were for me was now a bit tough. I just went by my instincts, thinking that she loved me but did not want to reveal so easily. The fact that I had not yet proposed her made me feel secure.

Siddhartha was back but I preferred Samit over him as far as love lessons were concerned. He finally guided me to propose her.

'*Saala, iss paar ya us paar, tu propose to kar*' He suggested.

It was 14th Jan. I was supposed to go to Dhanbad with Leena and Jaya. The keenness to go to Dhanbad was lost. Samit had well motivated me to its peak as I decided to propose her with a rose.

It was quite early in the morning or even the night was not over. I along with Samit went crazy as we planned to steal nice looking roses from plot no 16, the girl's address.

I was scared, but Samit was not. We jumped the black painted gate with little vibrating sound and then stopped for a while till the sound subdued. The garden had lots of roses of but were not practically visible in the darkness around.

Somehow we managed to get some Roses and happily returned back. We were so proud of our stealing ability as if we were able to steal a hard secured treasure or so.

'I will give her the rose and propose her when she will be there to see us off', I said to Samit as we returned.

He sarcastically smiled as if challenging my guts.

We were now waiting for the girls to come. It was around 8.00am when the girls arrived. In between the unintelligent discussions sometime, Samit announced 'You know, there is a boy in our coaching, who has fallen in love. He wants to propose her girl friend but scares. He even steals roses but can't give. Can anybody guess who?'

I became nervous hearing this and went out citing unnecessary reasons.

The story was quite clear now for everybody. My long face had now been squeezed like a lemon and I had lost all the courage I had developed to do the act of proposing her. To describe the situation better, I would rather say '*Meri to phat gayi thi*'.

Re-evaluating my decision to propose love, I finally settled on not to do so. Perhaps I was not brave enough.

I entered the room only to find that everyone was getting ready to move towards the Bus Stand. I was anxious of what all followed after I left. Samit make slowly indicating that in place of slowly that raised his right arm slowly that it was nothing serious. But that failed to inspire me.

Everyone was serious and I felt I was going to be butchered, first by Ruchi and then after reaching home. I was clearly seeing my love story inching towards death. My rapport back at home was also under scanner.

We reached the Bus Stand quite soon. Everybody was discussing something at ease but I was fairly lost and worried.

Slowly moving towards the bus, Leena waved her hands to others. Jaya followed with a giggle as usual in her cute petite face. Siddhartha gazed continuously towards Jaya, may be something had started brewing between the two.

Without disturbing Siddhartha, and refraining from any eye contact with Ruchi, I said, 'Bye' to Samit as he hopped inside an auto for his house. Ruchi slowly advanced towards the bus, chatting with Leena through the window. Girls anyways have a lot in store to chat.

Moving inside the nearly vacant bus, I placed my small bag over a seat. I took the weight out of my feet as I cocooned myself on the seat with my palm on my forehead. Apart from the worry of anything else, I was gloomier as I did not want to loose Ruchi.

It was still a while for the bus to depart. Succumbed by the ache within my mind, I came out of the bus for some fresh air of relief when I saw Siddhartha also chatting with the girls from the bus window.

With the company of my solitude, I parked my carcass at the rear end of the bus, placing my one leg on the number plate. My eyes took a wide view of the blue sky like a telescope, with my specs hanging on my shirts pocket.

Fiddling with the flowers I carried while leaving my room, I was cursing God for the situation. I was doing which I feel I was good at. Soon I found Ruchi stood in front of me from nowhere. A modest smile on her beautiful face was what she initiated with.

'Bye, you know even I am feeling like to go after seeing you all going home.' She said.

I remained silent ignorantly, speculating a thunderstorm. My head was down and hence were focused on her sandals as I could see her coming yet closer to me.

'*Phool Nahi Diye Na*'. She whispered in my ears and then looked straight into my eyes. I was intoxicated. '*Darpok ho ek number ke*'. 'Samit was speaking about you only, right?' She completed.

A sigh of respite was evidently noticeable on my face. I kept quiet, and then smiled to answer her questions. Taking the two roses out, I presented them in front of her, one red and the other white.

'And listen, I am not *darpok*. I just wanted to see...'

And before I could complete, she started laughing sarcastically. Her smile had all the metaphor needed to prove my appeal wrong.

Thinking for a while she took both the roses. Though I knew red rose indicate love, I was quite ignorant about the theories related to the white one. However I resisted myself from doing any research and was happy with whatever happened. I could see the same happiness in her as well. Now the question was how Leena portrays everything. I left it on god and leaped towards the gate as the cleaner shouted '*jaa badhaake....daiyen kaatke*'. *(KEEP LEFT AND MOVE ON)*.

Ruchi smiled and waved her hands across the bus as I could see her returning back with Siddhartha.

I reached home soon. It was a two days vacation, yet I was getting impatient to return back. I had developed the same feeling for Bokaro that I initially had for my home. Desperate to see and hear her voice, I called her once at the PCO, near their outhouse.

Thank God! The PCO owner was so cooperative.

As usual I was speechless and it was only a one way dialogue. 'Come soon and get something for me from there,' was something I could infer.

During all these episodes, my studies had taken a back seat. I knew it well that it was the only key to get Ruchi, but the practical realization of the same was missing.

We returned on serious notes, discussing about AIIMS, BHU and other colleges. Leena perhaps thought that it was better to motivate me for the medicals rather than to discourage me towards Ruchi.

We were there by the afternoon, but I still bunked the classes. So did Siddhartha. We closed our room and sat with a mood to discuss love and Siddhartha was the lecturer. In fact I could see in him some special feelings for Jaya, and may be that has ignited the fire in him.

There were mugs full of black tea with lemon as we had a gas stove by then. Outside was chilling and we had blankets on our laps, with books on top. It was a perfect *mise-e- place (preparations)* for the so called discussion.

'Are you in love with Ruchi?' He started.

'No yaar, its nothing like that. Just friends, but I enjoy her companionship.' I answered nodding my head in negation

He started smiling hearing the answer and kept quiet for a while. 'You know I got the same answer from Ruchi that day after you all left. Surprising,' He added.

'Anyways even if you have some other feelings for her, wipe it out as she claims that there can't be any possibility of her doing Love Marriage. I know it hurts, but that will be in the best of your interests.' He continued saying as I was deeply listening to him. I felt that the caffeine in the tea was providing him some spirits.

He continued with his lectures on the same topic until I intervened. 'Forget it. Tell me what about Jaya. That day I found you lost in her eyes.' I said as I focused on his face with my eyes wide open.

There were lines of smiles on his bashful face. I felt he was quite keen to hear this question and was ready to explode. He started as if a woman declaring her first pregnancy. Hiding his face he asked innocently, 'Do you think it is possible?'

'Yes, why not, but only if you want, and you are true to yourself. And as far as my instincts goes, I feel she likes you' I said with full confidence.

He was well satisfied by my answer as he wished something similar. Bullshits like that continued from both of us until we finally called off the day after dinner at around 1.40 am.

Though I did not paid much heed to his words owing to his nature and my past experiences with him, yet a doubt still prevailed about the relationship status I maintained with Ruchi. Nor was I brave enough to ask it to her.

I felt it better to live my life the way it was coming to me.

It was the next morning. Though I had nothing with me for Ruchi, I decided to buy a big Dairy Milk Chocolate for her. Actually the miser Aniruddha had turned into a spendthrift when it came to Ruchi. I bought the chocolate in the morning and gave it to her during our study at the princi's terrace.

Though a touch of romance was missing in the act yet I could see some changes in me as far as my views for Ruchi were concerned. Now I could compare her lips with rose petals, smiles with flowers and her charm better than any incandescence on earth. I wish I could tell them to her as well.

Now it was Jaya as well who used to come to the princi's terrace. Siddhartha also chipped in sometime because of her. It was more of a time pass than studies that we were actually doing there.

In no way I had it in my mind that Sid was very much in love with Jaya as I was selfishly lost in myself.

My idea of Sid being a kid was demolished when one morning I found his left arm slit with a blade. He had actually written a love letter to Jaya with his blood. 'Yes he did so.' I realized after pinching myself that I was not in dreams.

He was proud of his deeds as if he was Bhagat Singh and was taken for being hanged.

'Can you please hand it to Jaya?' He asked.

I took the letter in a flick and moved my eyes over it. Fully sentimental it was. I nodded to his query giving respect to his feelings. Providing some first aid, I had a glance of his face. I could witness the corporal pain in him and the anxiousness about the consequence of this stupid act.

Situation was tough. I had in my hand, the job of proposing Sid's love for Jaya and the weapon was a blood inked love letter by Sid. I was not even aware of the chemistry they shared.

Siddhartha tried to guide me with the procedure but I refused, and declared to continue only if I was allowed to do in my style. I had actually heard about token murderers, but I was token Loveguru.

I reached the coaching in style without Sid. Luckily Leena also bunked that day giving me full liberty to show my skills. I met them in an isolated staircase.

'And wassup girls? I started

'All is fine. What about you'. Both said in unison

'I am fine but', I paused and then continued

'You are looking fabulous Jaya. I mean your kohl lined eyes in your cute smiling face is all what I can see in the whole world. The dimple in your cheeks, lovely lips and above all your simplicity has ruined my sleep.'

Silence prevailed. Ruchi was shocked to hear that. So was Jaya, but she managed to reply.

'What happened to you? Are you alright? She said in her typical gesture.

I found Ruchi lost in some thoughts. Perhaps she was visualizing yet another Amitabh ji – Jaya ji tie up with herself as Rekhaji.

'Aur nahi to kya.' I said as I made an effort to prove my acting skills to myself.

'Jaya is beautiful, Jaya is pleasant, Jaya is pure, Jaya is this, and Jaya is that. Things like those are now more embedded in my memory rather than the Darwin's theory or Newton's Laws of motion. I continued with touch of frustration.

Smiles were back, Jaya with a bashful face and Ruchi with a sigh of relief.

'And you know what, when I suggested Sid to propose you, I never knew that he was such a true lover of yours' I said to Jaya with a wink.

'And I know that you also feel the same for him' I claimed.

Now Jaya was lost and I tried to seek a little help from Ruchi. I Signaled Ruchi to speak to Jaya.

She moved closer and placed her hand on her shoulders, and before she could say anything Jaya alleged, 'But why the hell he can't say anything'

'Because he scares that he would lose you and so he feels better to be your friend than nothing'. I advocated for Siddhartha.

My logics and petitions were not strong enough to motivate her. So I finally decided to take out the letter and hand it to her, which I was not in a mood to do. I was really scared about the possibilities to turn the game either way.

'See, this is why I say he loves you.' I said as I forwarded the letter to Jaya.

Without even completing the letter she broke into tears. Uncontrollable she was as she shouted 'it's my entire mistake'. The environment held stiff gravity.

Somehow, both I and Ruchi managed to cool her a little, though not totally and took her to our room. We left both the love birds in isolation and left the room for a walk.

Ruchi dared me not to do anything similar as she does not like it.

By uniting two lovebirds I was now their favorite and was a big Hero for Ruchi at least.

Girls departed, Siddhartha was happy and I was satisfied. But I was still wondering that a T-20 match of Sid was better than the five days test match I was playing.

AS IN MOVIES

Days passed on as I could see Jaya getting closer to Ruchi and Leena moving away. I was probably the reason. Leena was more formal to me than earlier. Still we five used to do things together.

It was the full brigade. Leena, Sid and I were studying at the terrace, and Ruchi and Jaya were in the room. Fully concentrated on studies I was discussing some Chemistry Numerical. Failing to solve them, I wondered how Mr. Charles, Mr. Boyles and others could manage it.

In a little while Ruchi called for Leena. She actually wanted Leena to solve a physics problem for her. Leena tried but could not succeed. It was further referred to me. May be it was a plan by Ruchi to keep Leena happy as well.

'Please solve this for me '. Ruchi requested.

I was happy but momentarily. Soon I found that the numerical was tough enough to be cracked. But I did not want to ruin my rapport created around. I tried my level best and finally came out with a correct answer.

I was happy but I could not convince her with the process.

Sid entered as a villain and solved the same in no time and that too in a very simple manner. Even I was happy to learn that, but sad at the same time as I could not solve it like Sid in front of Ruchi.

'Which was an easy way to solve it'? He asked boastingly.

Though I knew that Sid solved it in an easy manner, I wanted the judgment in my favor. Perhaps i had started developing expectations from Ruchi.

After thinking for a while she replied, 'Bhai jaan'

I went out silently. Siddhartha was still inside the room chatting with Jaya. I returned in no time. With my face turned white, ear lobes red I asked Sid for the room keys.

'What happened to you all of a sudden'? He asked

'Nothing, just like that' I replied, unable to hide the moistness of my eyes behind the glass lenses.

I took the Keys and rushed down the staircases.

Everyone were normal, but Ruchi followed me shouting continuously

'Aniruddha' 'Aniruddha'......was something I could hear as the name echoed all around. I came up to the street and she followed with the same approach. Fearless, bold, and focused she was. The scene was quite filmi, but she had decided not to stop.

A comedy was infused in the whole serious scene when I found one of the *Dhobi* (washerman) caught me and said, '*Arey babu, tohar mehraru bula rahal ba'*(o dear your wife is calling). Anybody would have burst with that with his peculiar tone and innocence, but I was not moved. I was still feeling insulted. The *dhobi* could maximum managed me to stop from moving ahead.

Ruchi reached me and with her own volition hold my right arm from behind. Without saying anything, she pulled me through the streets, up to the stairs to a vacant classroom. I felt like being the piece montage as everybody was witnessing the drama, including our professors.

'So much temper you have. I knew it was going to hurt you, but have you ever thought why I said so.'

'I know you care for me, you are a very good friend of mine, and problems are shared with someone who is close. It was you and not Bhai Jaan, and that's why I did so. But you boys are so in sensible.'

She continued as I was doing only the hearing part of communication. Unable to justify myself why she was shouting at me, I preferred to keep quite.

She continued giving lectures, which ended up with tears rolling down her pink cheeks. Before I could speak something or put my handkerchief to wipe down her tears, the villain entered again. 'O SHIT, NOT AGAIN', I thought but I was late.

Sid entered with a bang. 'Manner less creature', I thought, but it did not affect him.

'Ruchi, don't waste your time in somebody who is so in sensible'. Sid suggested. I just wondered of his intentions.

'I think so'. Ruchi said in a slow voice as she went out with Sid.

Everybody left for the rooms. It was 1.00 pm. As we approached the girl's place, I went near Jaya and whispered in her ears, 'Tell Ruchi to come to my room'.

She conveyed and I got an instant but indirect answer. 'She will be there after the lunch', Jaya said.

I went to my room, but did not had my lunch, Sid had. I didn't speak to him as well. I was waiting for Ruchi to come to sort things out. I was afraid of Siddhartha.

It was around 3.30pm that we found Ruchi and Jaya enter the room. Both went direct to Sid and soon I found Jaya and Sid leaving the room. Ruchi was quiet, sitting on Sid's bed. She took one of his books and started turning pages. She was not reading actually, just waiting for me to initiate talk. Girls generally feel they end up with less importance if the approach is from their side.

Trying to console her, I started, 'Did you have your lunch'?

'Yes I did.' She responded shortly.

Unaware of how to persuade girls, I went closer and sat in

the bed beside her. I wished if this part of love could be taught in a coaching, then I would have been the first to enroll myself.

'Can I ask you some simple questions?' I asked innocently.

She winked her eyes and nodded her head indicating affirmation.

'Who is the person you love the most' I asked after a pause. Though my intension was to create seriousness, but I failed as I found Ruchi answering the not so easy questions with ease.

'Minu-my sister.'

'Apart from her'

'My parents'

'No, I mean someone out of your family'. I asked as a naïve.

'Hmm… Then it's Zeba. You know her na.'

'And in Bokaro'

She thought for a while and said, 'Jaya'.

Though I was expecting my name right from the first question, I could not see it even in the last one. An expectation of Grade 'A' ended up in a failure. I was in no mood to appreciate her opinion. With my sunken face, I offered her a cup of tea and went ahead to prepare it.

Lost in the sorrow, I never noticed that Ruchi came closer to me. She switched off the gas stove which was making noise and hesitantly hold my hand and said 'Sorry'.

I looked at her like a coma patient. Every time I feel I have lost Ruchi, and I had regained her, she looks even more beautiful. With my eyes wide open I could see her smiling. And the smile was sufficient enough to cheer me up. Spontaneous changes were visible on my face.

'I am Sorry. I should have been thoughtful and considerate enough at that situation. Was going to set things right but Saala Siddhartha…. He always has to come at the wrong time'

'Thank God, he is not near now'. I said with satisfaction

'You know, I am very hungry. Can we have our lunch?' I asked.

Her mouth remained wide open hearing the same for a while. 'But why the hell have you not had your lunch. It's 4 'O' clock and....'

'I was not hungry then. Anyways let's not waste time. Let me see what Chaterjee Da(our tiffin man) have sent for me'

'Shut up you stupid. I can well understand why you didn't have your food. Come with me.' She started dragging me towards the Tiffin box. Opening the case she shifted the rice to a dish and poured some fish curry into the rice, and mixed it well. She looked for a spoon around and lifted a scoop to place it in my mouth. With no glass tumblers around, she served water to me in a mineral water bottle. The curry was good as usual but today it tasted exceptional.

She stared at me continuously as I relished the food.

'You know sometimes I am very confused about your persona.' She stated.

'Why?' I asked taking a fish bone out of my mouth.

'Because you still doubt that who the person I love most is? And so I doubt what you feel at different situations.' She said quickly. I felt the masticated mixture of fish, rice and curry sliding down my esophagus.

I was not quite sure what did she intended to speak, but I knew she wanted me to show proximity, though not physical yet verbal.

Rinsing my hands, I went near her, sat beside. Placed my hand on her chin to lift it up and looked into her eyes. 'I need your help....for.....the chemistry

And before I could complete the villain was back. 'Dhan te Nan' he shouted at the door.

We quickly gave space to ourselves. Jaya came in. 'Shall we leave'. She suggested.

Ruchi looked towards me and left without uttering anything else. I ran but could manage to say Sorry only. I repented within myself as to why I did not propose in a direct 'I LOVE YOU'.

My inability to make my points clear was now visibly evident. Ruchi stopped coming to the Princi's terrace for the morning session. Though a regular chat was not seized, yet the intensity was lost. I also felt many a time that she wants to propose from her side, but she pretended to be annoyed with me. She was actually not good at pretending.

It was Jaya now in the terrace with me. Frustrated with the physical chemistry numerical, I threw my book aside.

'What's wrong with you?' she asked.

Unmoved by her question, I kept quiet. It's not only this chemistry which is disturbing you; I feel there is one more chemistry.' She claimed as she picked up the book and came closer.

'You can discuss your problems with me. I am your friend, and if you want I can be your secret bank as well.' she said

'You mean a lot to me. I feel I have got one more brother after coming here' She continued. Her words were sounding too filmi for me to respond. She tried a lot but failed to induce me with her sentimental dialogues.

She changed her stance and got more aggressive. 'What do you think I don't know things? I know what is killing you. It is related to Ruchi, more than anything else.' She explained.

I was trapped.

'See the change in your face hearing her name. You ask people to be bold, and see what you are. You are hiding facts to yourself.' She continued.

I was soon in a state of panicky. Jaya could have been a better lawyer than a doctor. Offering some mint (polo), she tried to cool me off and asked me in a very simple sweet and slow manner, 'Do you love Ruchi'?

Dumb stuck I was. Gaining confidence within I said 'Yes'.

'Yes', she repeated as she smiled.

'I mean it's more Yes than No' I replied bashfully.

'Does Ruchi also......'

'May be', she replied. It did not make me happy as I was willing to hear a confident 'Yes'.

I took some more mint from her and left for my room. I had to pack my bags for the next day trip to Dhanbad for Saraswati puja.

* * *

It was a lighter shade of dark as we returned to Bokaro. The class was on and we reached Bokaro late, thus preferred to do a group study. A focused study for a couple of hours and a short beak then, lifted the mood. Spring was at the doors. We planned for an outing together with Leena, Ruchi and Jaya. It was the first time I was going out with Ruchi to date her. It was my first date. Though it was in correct to call it a date but who cared.

The destination was CITY PARK. I was frequently seen in Denims by then. Unfamiliar about others, I only knew that my costumes were selected by Ruchi, though her dress was not by me. Girls generally believe they are better designers.

I woke up early in the morning. I made a lengthy itinerary for the whole day in a piece of paper. Just as Siddhartha woke up, I rushed to the bathroom. I was generally an aqua phobic and this issue increased to several folds in the winters. Half bucket was more than sufficient for me to bathe but the scene was different that day.

I came out and combed for almost half an hour, using all types of Gels Present in the room. I never had the habit of using them. Looking myself from all the possible angles I settled for one particular style that I thought would impress Ruchi the most. I was rather callous of all these otherwise.

I came out of my room in an off white Wrangler jeans and a white vest. I peeped outside the main gate to find whether Ruchi was coming. Actually she was supposed to bring me one of her stone wash navy blue shirt.

Yes, a girl's shirt, but I could not oppose to Ruchi's view on this. Quite possible that people thought that I was henpecked before marriage. Forget marriage, even before the first date!

Even Siddhartha tried his level best to look handsome. His plum cheeks were glowing as usual as he gave the credit to 'Seven Seas Cod Liver Oil Capsules'

Soon Ruchi evolved with the shirt in her hand. She was looking glamorous with a navy blue skirt and a pink top. Leena and Jaya followed her to our room. In no time the desolated room had turned to a lively stage.

As I inserted the shirt within my jeans, I could see wrinkles on Ruchi's eyebrows. It was a message for me to not do so.

I later realized that short shirts are better out. During all these times I could see the girls still in search of the fineness in the application of various colored chemicals on their face and lips. On every such situation my father's quote echoes in my ears and mind. 'Twenty per cent of a women's life is spent in front of the mirror'.

After a long wait we finally decided to leave. We were five in numbers so I suggested Leena, Jaya and Siddhartha to depart in an auto and we would follow in some time. I was happy to convince them and so was Ruchi. But before we could leave, Sharan Bhaiya arrived and directly said,

'Are you both going somewhere? Take the Keys.' He handed over the scooter keys to me as he said so.

I looked at Ruchi's eyes and smiled. She said a small 'Thank You Bhaiya' to Sharan Bhaiya.

I parked my butt on the seat of the Bajaj Chetak Scooter and kicked it to a start. With the sound of the ignition, Ruchi sat as the pillion with both legs on the same side, crossing each other. I slowly released the clutch and changed the gears to perfection as I accelerated the vehicle to a moderate speed. I wished Ruchi to hold me but she preferred the rod beside.

We reached the park in a smooth ride. Others were shocked to see us coming in a scooter. Ruchi detailed them with the story as I parked the scooter.

We entered the park in group of five but soon it was divided into three and two. It was a different scene this time. Just after entering the park Siddhartha took Jaya aside and in no time they were invisible. I had no other choice to than to give company to both Ruchi and Leena.

My itinerary was crushed and I was helpless. Though Ruchi was happily chatting with Leena yet I could see the urge in her eyes to go private. In around one hour or so Ruchi started moving alone. Her face was shrunk but she did not say anything.

Leena could read her sentiments as well and said,

'Go and speak to her. She is feeling lonely and depressed. She wants your company.'

'And You' I asked.

'I will be fine here and after all you also want her company'. She smiled as she said so.

I stood up slowly from the cultivated grasses and moved towards Ruchi. She was standing near the pond.

'She is my sister, Right. I can't leave her alone. I hope you understand. You know she only pushed me to speak to you now' I said as I stood beside her.

'It's okay. I can understand.' She said as she waved her hands to Leena to call her but she refused.

We sat together as I started to boast of her beauty. 'You know I am the happiest person on earth today.'

'Why is it so?'

'Because I have realized my dream. You are my dream. I want you to be mine. I want to live with you, eat with you, play with you and even die with you. I don't know about love, but if this is love then I love you' I said in a well rehearsed tone.

So finally I had proposed my love to her. She looked continuously towards my eyes and I to her full face. 'I am sorry if that did hurt you.' I said to safeguard myself.

She smiled and turned her face.

'Ruchi' I called her name. She turned towards me as she heard that.

'Do you also feel the same?' I asked hoping for a positive reply.

'I don't know. Shaayad Haan' she said with a shy face.

All these things were quite obvious but just it was not happening. I wondered why there was a process for everything. If you can send the ball to boundary that mattered, rather than what stroke you played. I still remembered that the answer was not the only thing which was important in a numerical. It was the process as wel.

Unable to bear the boredom Leena finally reached us. We were happy that our conversation was over by that time. She took the camera out and clicked me and Ruchi together. It was our first photograph as a couple. My hesitation to show proximity with Ruchi in front of Leena was quite evident from the Photograph when prints came out.

THE SMOKE OF DRAMA

Things to follow were not normal. A steep change in the behavior of Ruchi was found right in next few days.

She turned her face back seeing me. Answering to my queries and speaking to me, were out of question. By virtue of her nature, I felt she was pretending to be angry with me, but this time it was no drama.

Without delay I could investigate the reason as Jaya proved out to be a real support for me. She was apprehensive as she called me and said, 'Don't take her wrong. Actually our landlord had complained against her to her parents and they were here the next day. Her father was so annoyed, that he wanted to take her back to Dhanbad before the completion of the course. We persuaded her father, but he settled only by giving Ruchi a last chance.' She said them all in a stretch.

I was neither able to think anything nor speak. Finally I managed to utter the name, 'Ruchi! What is she saying now?'

'She would probably do as per her father. She is actually bound to follow them.' Jaya said after thinking for a while.

'But how will I live…..I mean she as well……….You are the best person who knows everything between us. Tell me.' I tried to convey my distress through broken sentences. Tears tried to overflow from my eyes and I never bothered to stop them.

'I can't let it happen. I will not let her move away from my life so easily.' I said gathering all the confidence, wiping away my tears. 'I hope you are with me'. I completed with a mark of expectation on my face.

She smiled in affirmation. 'I owe it to you dear. It's my privilege.'

'Okay fine. Tell me whether the complain involves my name as well or just normal complain?' I asked with anxiety.

'Why?' She asked wondering, whether I was scared or so.

'Don't worry. I am just guessing that if my name is not there the work ahead can be easy. I hope you got it.' I said clearing her doubts.

'Now, can you manage to get Ruchi to speak to me once?' I proceeded with my plan.

'I will do that as soon as I can.' She said and left for her room. I had a very big challenge in front of me now. Even calculus seemed to be peanuts in front of that. Looking towards the sky I questioned, 'WHY, WHY ME', and finally I brought the head down with a smile. Perhaps I had got the answer.

My Hanuman Jee wanted to test me. He also wanted me to be strong enough to face these issues.

It was six days that we did not meet or rather spoke to each other. Valentine's Day was two days away. I hoped that Jaya would make it to that day, but she failed. Ruchi did not want to meet me at any cost. Even I could not manage to speak to her at the coaching institute.

Leena, Siddhartha, Jaya, all knew of my condition but were helpless. I had lost all my concentration in studies and my thin frame looked even thinner. Actually I had stopped eating. It was not a hunger strike but as if nothing went down my throat.

Though not expected, but it worked. The news of my condition reached Ruchi and finally she decided to reach me. A little of the complain issue had subsided by then, still she took utmost protection to come to my room. It was the full brigade there, but they left us in isolation.

'Don't you love me anymore?' was a straight forward question at her. 'What's wrong with you?' I added.

A silence prevailed. I was looking up for an answer and she was perhaps drafting the same within herself.

'I don't know anything about that.' She paused. 'But I know I can't love you and marry you because of the orthodoxy existing in my family. So I think it's better to seize this emotional drama before it makes our life bitter.'

It was the first time that I was seeing the bold and the positive Ruchi so much down under.

'But will this not hurt you?' I asked an obvious question.

'It will but I will overcome that in some days and feel you will also do that. Actually the relation that we are sharing is called INFATUATION. I agree that it happens but it erases as well.' She tried to convince me and prove her logic right. Someone had impressively motivated her in the opposite direction.

'Don't act childish. You know how much I love you, and so do you. Have you forgotten all our plans for our future? The future which both of us had dreamt of, together to live in.' Tears almost came out but I resisted as I said so.

Students In coaching said that my hypothalamus is over reactive. May be it was, but this time, it had obvious reasons to show sentiments.

'Eat food and live well. See me, have I gone crazy like you? You will have to be practical enough. And not to forget, study well. I want you to crack the Medicals anyhow.' She lined up lectures as I was still wishing that she was pretending.

But she was not. I expected her to take some food out of the Tiffin box and place it in my mouth as no one was around, but it did not happen. Instead she said a formal 'bye' and left.

I failed to convince her. To convince that I was the guy made for her or rather the fact that we are made for each other. She otherwise had de motivated me to love her any more.

The coaching had only twenty days left to get over. I was back to the old initial phase, tensed about selection in medical college and tortured by home sickness. I gradually knew that Ruchi was no more in my life, but still my heart did not want to believe that. Her smile was still fresh before my eyes. Jaya, I knew was feeling sorry for me and was still my source of inspiration if any I had, to get Ruchi back.

The group was shattered. We never used to meet together as before. Leena had planned to leave the coaching well in advance as she felt that she was not able to study there anymore. Siddhartha's classes were only ten days left so he had also started packing bags.

Siddhartha also did not cruised in his love story for long as some of his father's colleagues spotted him with Jaya and mocked him. Chances of Ruchi's father being one of them can't be over ruled.

Siddhartha's mother knew about his affair with Jaya.

I had often heard her saying, 'Concentrate on your studies rather than thinking of MAHARANI'. That was the name Sid's mother had christened Jaya with.

Jaya on the other hand knew of all these and took things sportingly. A sensible girl she was.

Beyond expectation, one sunny afternoon Siddhartha's mother and aunt came in a self owned Ambassador car to take him back. Though both the ladies were too good in their interrogative skills, it was tough for them to extract facts, taking me in remand.

'*Na kakima, aami oto kichhu jaani na*'.(No I don't know much about that). I said as I defended me and Sid both.

Siddhartha hugged me and gave his address and phone number only at the last time.

'Bye' said Siddhartha and '*Aasbe*' (Do visit us) said his mother as they left for Dhanbad.

I went as an ambassador of Siddhartha to Jaya and presented all that I had for her. Ruchi was around as well. Jaya's eyes said that she was both shocked and sad, but was well under control as they had already planned what to do next.

'Any special comments on me from his mother?' Jaya asked.

'No, this time she was more concentrated on Maharaja than Maharani.' I tried to bring a curve on her lips.

'But Bhai jaan should have met you once before leaving. Though his mother was there, but if he wished he could have done so.' She said to Jaya but I felt it was directed to my ears as well.

A stern look followed by a sarcastic smile was my answer. Both were intelligent enough to interpret that. 'Look who is saying' type expression was conveyed to them.

I went back to my room or Rana's room rather. He was my kin now. Knowing everything around, he tried to cheer me up and we walked ahead to city centre.

'Slambook' he suggested me to buy one.

'But why', I pondered. 'Now that I don't want to remember anything happened here at Bokaro and carry them forward in life why do I need that?' I placed my strong logic.

'It's always better to end up things in a positive note. Part with Ruchi as a friend as she wants, rather than a foe. May be.........' he suggested and left me guessing the text that he didn't spoke out.

I could perhaps see some miracle in those blank lines because it propelled me to buy a Slam Book. We took an auto to return back, but throughout the way I was thinking the best possible way to use it.

I took the slam book and on the very first page I wrote about myself as per the questionnaire put forward. The most important thing was I had still written 'RUCHI' as my crush and favorite girl both.

Next was Rana. He did his best to answer the questionnaire and about me his work was rather diplomatic. 'NEVER FALL IN

THE SAME ENTANGLEMENT OF LIFE FROM WHICH YOU
ARE TRYING TO EXTRICATE FROM, ESPECIALLY G____L.'

His intentions were quite clear to me. He tried to hit Ruchi
knowing the fact that her nick name was GUPUL, which could
well fit in the gap.

Without thinking much about the consequences, I handed
over my Slam book to Jaya so that all the girls should fill what
they feel about me, though I did not stated Ruchi's name in
particular.

The night passed in speculation of all the possibilities
to be filled in the slam book only taking Ruchi into account.
Sometimes I was walking alone in the desolated lanes of the
colony; otherwise a cup of black tea provided me the company. I
finally surrendered to tiredness at around 5.00am.

Not even able to complete half of the desired sleep, I was
awake by Jaya and Ruchi sharp at 8.00am. I generally don't
entertain people when I feel sleepy, but Ruchi.................
Sorry, I never wanted to take chance..

'Still sleeping!' Jaya exclaimed.

I could not pronounce a word. My greasy face, moist lips,
scattered hair and sunken eyes suggested that I still wanted to
sleep.

'Get up. Its 8 'O' clock' Jaya said as she came near me
and shook my body to bring me active. 'Freshen up soon', she
ordered.

'What were you dreaming about? Certainly a girl.' She
questioned only to answer herself with a mischief.

I quickly ran my eyes down my trousers owing to find out
the reason for her confidence. Thank god. It was just an obvious
claim and nothing that I was scared of.

All what her words did was it took me completely out of
sleep. I leaped towards my tooth brush as I saw Jaya adjusting
my crinkle sheet of my bed. During all these Ruchi was just a

silent spectator and her silence broke only when I offered her a cup of tea.

'Thank you', she said. As this visit of theirs was not expected, I could well smell some reaction in her particularly with Rana's comments.

She took my slam book out and placed beside her. I could not resist myself from lifting it. Flipped the pages of the book and settled on with a girl called Anubha Agarwal, trying to misguide her that I was actually looking for her comments.

'Can I speak to Rana?' She asked as her eyes suggested that she was hurt.

'Yes, but why.' I said as I rotated my eyes between the two of them, pretending to be naïve.

'Please,' said Ruchi. It was more of an order than request. I felt chocked like a constipation patient as I directed Ruchi's demand to Rana's servant.

Rana came out late, maybe he was playing some mind game, Smiling and proud as usual. He could well read the temperament of the person he speaks to, like a focused salesman. 'Did somebody remember me?' he said as he entered.

Though the girls never spoke to him directly, Ruchi was set to do that.

'What all do you know about me and my relation with Aniruddha. You not even know me nor my problems and feelings. I think you should consider everything before coming to any conclusion.' She filed the petition and announced the judgment herself.

Staring at Jaya's face I was seeking some intervention from her side to bring situation to normal. 'Forget it. he must have written it with some other intensions' Jaya said as she tried to put some ice on Ruchi's rage.

This short time was sufficient enough for Rana to organize his speech. 'Sorry.', he paused. Sorry that I commented on you, but as far as my understanding goes, this boy loves you a lot. I have seen the transformations in his life from the day you trailed out. When you knew that you can't cruise in your love life why the hell you did spoil someone's dream.' Rana completed in a very straight forward verse.

Ruchi ran out of the room crying. Jaya followed. I looked at Rana, but he was smiling as usual in the tense environment. I decided to visit the girls but postponed till a part of the sentiments subdued.

Seeing every stance failing I decided to go by my instincts and knocked at their room in the evening. My main motto was to say Sorry and close things off as I was leaving on the next day.

Jaya opened the door and closed it as I entered. Perhaps they knew what was I there for. Ruchi, though was sad, yet her sob was not visible outside.

Killing the silence around she said, 'You have created a mess in my life. You don't know the true meaning of love. I know my father, and I am bound to follow his wish. I wish I would have never met you.' She said very bluntly.

I kept looking at Ruchi expecting some words of solidarity from her but spoke when she did not. 'You must be feeling it was me behind Rana's act. But I was not, because I LOVE YOU, and I don't hurt those whom I love. Do you understand that? Though it is also true that now also I want you to return back, but I will try to move out of you if it keeps you happy.'

'Anyways I am leaving tomorrow evening and I am expecting a little help from you all in packing my bags' I said as I wanted to cool things off and also probably because I wanted to see Ruchi once more for the last time.

'Haan Haan, we will be there.' Jaya replied with a smile.

I kept the tea made by Jaya, almost cold by this time and left with a bye.

I came back home heartbroken. Tried to yell and shout aloud. Sometimes I wished to smoke away all my agony, sometimes drink and forget all sorrows. But I virtually did not manage to do either of them. Thanks to my sweet and strict upbringing on these lines. I finally ended up writing scraps in a piece of paper. I never knew it would come out to be a nice and sentimental love letter.

The sleepless night rolled on to a bizarre morning. With a still persisting hang over of the so called journey of love, I had finally planned my way of exit from Ruchi's Life. Keeping my love letter in my diary as a bookmark, I left to bring my clothes from the Dhobi (washerman). The doors were not locked, just caressing each other to give an expression of someone inside.

I returned back with dizziness in my eyes only to realize that both the girls had read the letter. Though my intention was to make them read but in a different manner, probably after I leave Bokaro.

They were in the stance to move out of the room with Jaya not smiling, unlike as usual and Ruchi crying. My face was evidently nervous with no support from Jaya's look.

The well drafted letter on an Oblong note book page was now rolled all along like a bamboo stick. I had all of again did my best to take the bamboo out of a moving truck and put it in my ass. 'Why the hell do I require writing and giving all bullshit theories of love when everything was over? We had broken up, just the formality remained.' I said to myself.

'What happened? Why are you crying?' I said portraying both my innocence and ignorance.

Jaya turned towards Ruchi's hand which was carrying the letter to convey reasons. Ruchi was still sobbing, and her tears were falling on the letter like pearls. Her deep breaths as she inhaled volumes of air through her nostrils indicated that she tried hard to stop herself from sobbing.

With no answers reaching my eardrums, I moved towards Ruchi and tried to wipe out her tears, something I could not do in the past due to Siddhartha. I was also acting on my own script what I had written in that letter. It would have been a good screenplay if all these stills would have been put into motion picture.

'Come inside and tell me what happened. Why crying?' I said in a soft voice showing my empathy.

'*Chhod ke to jaa rahe ho*' She said in Hindi with yet another throb of sob. I ran short of expressions with that. Trying to guess the gist of those lines I asked the maid to make some tea for us.

Though the letter had done its share of task, yet a perfect decision of my destiny was still not declared. The tea was over and Ruchi was comparatively normal. Of course it was a spark of hope but I was actually in dilemma about her confused persona.

'Fine, tell us all what has to be packed?' asked Jaya.

'Everything, including me.' I smiled.

Ruchi tried to speak but did not. I was still in a dilemma as to how encash the tears in her eyes to some more love quotes for me.

'What time is your bus to depart?' Jaya asked.

'Any time you both get me ready. I mean I will decide it later when to go. It's Dhanbad only'. I replied.

'Frankly speaking, I am not willing to go…..today at least.' I said after a pause.

'Then why are u going? She asked with exclamation

'Just because, someone never stopped me from going.' I reasoned.

'You never know, 'your someone', might be willing to stop you, but perhaps can't afford to do so.'Jaya transformed the scene even more dramatic.

The ball was in Ruchi's court now. But she preferred to speak only to change the topic.

'I have told Chaterjee Da to drop both our Tiffins here. We will have our lunch here with you today. Let's start packing things, there are many.' Ruchi said as I saw her folding the letter back into square and keeping it in her tunic's pocket.

She started with stacking the books. Each of those books had her name scribbled in almost all the pages. Sometimes 'I love you' suffixed it; otherwise it was in an equation with my name. She knew all these and so never tried to flip the pages. Jaya joined her as well.

Shelves were getting vacant and bags were getting filled up. I tried to supervise them but my suggestions had no place in their processes. Environment inside the room held gravity as both I and Ruchi were mute. Jaya's giggles were heard in short frequencies.

'You guys are good in maintaining the house. Your wives will be happy.' Jaya said

'Of course yes and hence I can see smile on your face.' I replied to check Ruchi's reaction. Though she smiled, it was for Jaya.

I rushed to the bathroom to bath and came back quickly as usual. They were over with the books and stationeries by then and were into my garments. I could see them laughing over. My boxers were perhaps the reason.

Cutting their laughter short, they decided to leave for their room for taking bath.

'We will be there in an hour. Wait till we come and we will have food then.' Jaya suggested and they left.

I had nothing to do in the next couple of hours. The letter also was with them now. My mind was unable to think. Perhaps it was kept in a cold storage at -18 degree Celsius to be used later.

They returned at quarter to three. We hurriedly gulped the food with the feeling as if it was a medicine. Before I could wrap up the newspaper on which we had placed our plates and ate, Jaya was vanished.

'Where is jaya?' I asked to Ruchi.

'Off late, she remembered some work and left. She will be back after some time' Ruchi replied.

Pre meditated it was, and I had no problems in realizing that.

Once again after a long time it was just two of us. My heart beat was increasing and so was her's, but it had no relation with our testosterone or estrogen levels. I felt as if someone had injected Adrenaline in us.

We came closer with the distance being less than a foot long. 'Ruchi,' The name came out of my mouth in a very low pitch. She turned towards me to pay attention.

'I can understand everything and I know that so do you. You miss me a lot, may be more than I do. It will be tough to live without you. I don't know how I will. Your face, smile and innocence will be my saviors. Thanks for being 'MY RUCHI' all these days.' I completed.

I took a pen with a red ink from around and scribbled I LOVE YOU on her left palm. A warm kiss over the same followed.

She took the pen from me and on the diary started writing.

> Can you hear it
> Beautiful one
> When love calls,
> The power of love
> Keeps calling you
> *Come O LOVE*

'Never keep this away from you.' She ordered.

Moving towards her bag, she removed a gift out to present it to me. Small, rectangular and wrapped in gift paper; tough to guess. 'With love', it stated.

As she moved out of the room as I could see Jaya standing outside from the window. Ruchi showed her palm to her. Jaya's usual smile was bigger this time. Both entered the room again.

I was all set to leave. My baggage had increased three folds since I came to Bokaro. One suitcase, two big shoppers and a small handbag, all full to the extent of overflowing. Jaya helped me out with the handbag and me and Ruchi shared the rest as we walked down the lane to the bus stand.

Differences were sorted out but the psychological pain of the two was quite obvious. But apart from that some corporal pain was also visible in the eyes of Ruchi owing its link to her hands.

Her hand which was holding one of the overweight big shopper had turned red and she was continuously trying to hide the pain.

Walking lost in my own world; I could discover the situation off late.

'Are you mad or what, can't you say that it is heavy. What do you want to prove with that?' I shouted continuously as I managed to snatch the big shopper from her and placed it on the road.

An idiot look surfaced on her face which she tried to envelop with a fake smile. More fake than an air hostess gives to the boarding passengers.

Guilty of being responsible for all, I checked for some coolant nearby. Maximum I could locate was a PANIPURI WALA. I rushed to get some water from him.

'*Bhaiya thoda sa paani dena, jaldi se.*' I requested.

'*Paani waani nahin hai.*' He replied irritated.

'*Hai kaise nahin, seedhi baaat samajh mein nahin aati hai.*' I said as I lifted his tangy soup pot and ran towards Ruchi.

He kept shouting and others including Jaya laughing. I did not know whether they were laughing at me or my work. Insensibly I poured the tangy water into Ruchi's hand. She licked her hand to show that the pain was arrested.

'*Itna mast pani phenkne se accha pila dete.*' She said amusingly. Smiling at each other we finally reached the bus depot.

With a hope that my last words can do miracle I started but could end up in a stammer. 'R..R..Ruchi, can you give me something?'

'What'?

'My Ruchi back to me. You know I need her. Please try at least.'

The bus arrived giving me no time to get the response. Hurriedly I was pushed into the bus and it departed in a flick. I could only helplessly stare at the waving hands of Ruchi from the bus till it was vague.

LET THE CURRY SIMMER
DHANBAD

*L*ost, all along, throughout the journey I reached home. Everybody was happy to see me back and I too tried to show similar emotions.

Too inquisitive about the gift, I opened the packet in solitude. It was a crystal souvenir enchanting the friendship quotes. I showed them to everybody. The friendship was 'with love', I wondered.

'She is a very sober girl. I really like her. Her gift shows that she has a good up bringing as well. Otherwise girls now days....... they gets ripened just at birth.' My dadi said.

I don't know what others did but I could not conclude anything from that. I was just a bit happy that if things materialize from her end, it would not be a big problem to get it sanctioned from my house, because in my house my dadi was the King and Queen both.

I turned towards my Uncle's PCO as I had to call Ruchi about my safe reach. We did not have any telephone at our house those days. Call it our callousness or from the department of Telecommunications.

Just as I reached the PCO my uncle exclaimed, 'OK you have

reached, give Ruchi a call. Poor girl is frantically tensed about you.'

'Too many calls for you, haan!!!!!!' my uncle smiled

'Obviously, get me a phone at house as well' I smiled back.

I dialed the number and completed the communication in words rather than in sentences. Too formal in front of my uncle.

'We are getting a parallel connection to this number tomorrow at our house for the time being'. He boasted as if he managed to clinch a big deal with the U.S senator.

The week ended in re adjustment in my house. I also had to visit Siddhartha to return few of his stuffs back. No communication with anyone happened in all these days. Procrastination was the reality but I held the studies guilty.

Finally I reached Siddhartha. He was waiting for me right on the main road to pick me up. as soon as he noticed me he quickly ran towards me and hugged me.

'*Kaisa hai Bhai*' he said.

'*Acchha re*' I replied.

'Any idea about the girls'

'None, since I left Bokaro.'

'Let's call them today.' He suggested.

We rushed towards the PCO to call them. Siddhartha dialed the number 0654224396. It was the PCO beside their outhouse.

The call was received by Jaya itself.

'Jaya you, what are you doing there'

'We just tried calling Aniruddha, but her aunt said that he left for your house. Later we tried calling you but every time your mother was picking up the call. I was afraid to hear MAHARANI.' She completed.

'Yes Aniruddha is with me only but how are you'

'I am fine but first give the phone to Aniruddha. Ruchi wants to speak to him.'

Siddhartha granted me the phone killing his desire to express his feelings to Jaya, stored since last couple of weeks.

'Hello', 'Ruchi'. I called after a pause.

'Aniruddhha' She replied stretching my name.

'Yes, Yes, tell me what you wanted to say.' I said unable to keep patience.

'Actually, I can give you what you said that day.' She said them all at a stretch in a shy tone. I needed no more hints to understand that it was again a reunion from her side.

Though I was experienced with these situations in the past, yet I did not have the skills to manage it. Nervousness was incorporated with ecstasy. I turned mute and felt once again as if a Jinnie came to turn my wish true.

Though I was speechless, yet my eyes were able to speak everything. But useless it was. The telephone could not capture that. I had finally won a prize in lottery, which I was missing every time just by the last digit.

Siddhartha took over the phone to continue. It was emotions everywhere, I and Sid here in Dhanbad and Jaya and Ruchi there at Bokaro.

I came back home just after a formality visit to Sid's home. His mother did her best to preach us about the necessities of studying unaware of the fact that her son was still in love with Maharani.

I came back home with the greatest happiness and biggest smile on my face. My chachi called me aside and shoot me a question point blank. 'Who is this Ruchi? The same girl who gave you that gift'

Though she was Chachi(aunt) to me yet my relation was more friendly type. Thanks to the small age gap between us.

'She called five times since evening. Her words had a lot of desperation to speak to you.' Chachi said teasingly.

I went away unanswered. Generally I do such things when I am nervous.

∗

Ruchi's small sentence on the other day over phone was sufficient for me to miss her. I could see her face now even in the algae and fungi of my textbook. Even parathas served to me were looking oval.

'Can you relieve your kaka from the booth for his breakfast?' My chachi asked as she served some crispier aloo bhujiyas on my plate.

'Sure.'

A smile generated on her face. People are wrong in saying that love evades after marriage, I concluded. They were married for six years now.

I moved towards the STD booth with a Biology book in my hand. Happy to help like the Hutch dog.

'Just half an hour.' Chachi reminded me that it was a good help considering my exams at door.

I went ahead without bothering to answer towards the booth.

'Nice parathas and Aloo bhujiyas are waiting for you Trivedi Jee. I think little priority should be given to them as well.' I beamed as I approached Bhai Kaka in the booth.

'That's fine, but what about the booth?' was a straight question.

'I will be here.' I replied confidently. 'I know that one local call is for two rupees and even STD codes are known to me. Bombay-022, Delhi-011, Calcutta-033……….' I continued till I said all I knew. It had more of an intension to show off my cheeky knowledge rather than convincing him.

'Yes but that's not all.' He smiled

'My name is Aniruddha Trivedi and I am your nephew, I think that would be all.' I said boastingly for both of us; something he liked the most.

His sixteen sets of tooth were visible as his hands rose to his moustaches to curl them up. His chest might have inflated from thirty four inches to forty inches, I wondered.

As he left the PCO was in auto-pilot. The place was soon

deserted as not so many people preferred to call during peak pulse rate hours.

The high pitched ring tone of the BSNL phone distracted me from the little concentration I could gather at the 'myopia' of my textbook. The sharp tone left me with no other choice than to receive the call before the second ring.

'Hello.' I said

'*Hello Corner se bol rahe hain*'

'*Haan Boliye*'

'*Thoda sa bagal wale Sahu Jee ko bula dijiye. Bagal mein unka khaini ke dukan hai.*'

Before I could visualize the person called for, I envisaged an idea. Yes, to call Ruchi. 'Why the hell it did not come in my mind earlier.' I said to myself.

Though being co-operative enough I called Sahu Jee, yet I was desperate to see his call getting over. I jumped on to dial the same number dialed by Siddhartha that day without paying heed to Sahu Jee's 'Thanks' to me.

'Aniruddha here. Can you please ask Ruchi or Jaya from next plot to give me a call' I requested over the phone. I chose not to give their business status unlike Sahu Jee's kin.

'Yes, why not.' A co operative voice entered my ears. I put the phone back with the expectation of a quick call back.

Right I was, as within minutes the phone rang again. My 'Hello' got the response in form of silence. I was sure it was Ruchi.

'How are you.' I asked

'How did you know that it was me?' she questioned to answer my previous question.

'My heart said so.' I said simply. Though I wanted to insert some nice dialogues, but failed to recollect. There was no one to proxy as well.

'*Kaise ho?*'

'Fine till now, but won't continue if you don't call me daily.'

'Here, on this number.' I completed.

'But uncle! Isn't he around?'

'No he is not and will not be there daily during this period.' I detailed her with the Breakfast plan. I could hear her giggle over the phone as if we had planned for our honeymoon. We ended up short though happy to plan our regular conversation.

It had been customary by then to chat with Ruchi. I was clever enough to disguise the actual reason to attend the PCO. Bhai Kaka was also getting sufficient time to attend to his Youth Congress Party. He constantly received resilience from the home, yet he managed to be the Youth Congress President, though not in his youth days. I always wondered why this Youth wing of these parties start it in schools portraying a bright career in hypocrisy ahead.

Examinations were approaching and everyone was tensed. So did I. The coaching had offered all the students a final free mock test for the PMT. I decided to gauze where I stand via that examination and also to meet Ruchi after long.

It was a nice Sunday morning. The same THE EXPRESS bus carried me upto Bokaro in a jerky journey over the NH-32. Though the government claims the road to be like some Bollywood actress's cheek; marks of pimples and Small pox appear on them in no time. I was waiting outside the gate of the girl's plot to meet them as going inside might invite the *Buddha* Landlord for yet another job in his retired life. Yes, to complain…..

Nobody was around there except some mynahs chirping.

One for sorrow,

Two for joy,

Three for letter

Four for Guest

I remembered, as I saw the mynahs. Ruchi used to recite upto number twenty as I wondered about the origin of these quotes. Girls were visible only after a long wait. Clad in a Salwar Kameez she was looking simple and elegant. In all these days of companionship with me she had perhaps studied that I like her in traditional costumes as they cover you a whole lot, but not in a burqa type though.

She came out murmuring some equations and moved towards the coaching recapitulating some tough Biological terms to pronounce. Though Jaya greeted me, her words were masked by 'Kleinfelter's Syndrome' and 'Down's Syndrome' coming of Ruchi's mouth.

Ruchi's acting skills were really poor. Her happiness was evident from her eyes but she pretended to be bothered for examination. Without much conversation we entered the examination rooms and were diversified as per the seats allocated.

Putting pressure on all the grey and white matter we had within our skull, we came out after the examination. We were pretty satisfied as the questions were comparatively simpler.

With an expectation of a nice chat from Ruchi, I started with a wrong Subject. 'The questions were not at par with the ones of PMT's right!' I claimed.

'That doesn't bother me. What bothers me now is for how long you are here? She said in a reserved tone and smiled later.

'Evening perhaps.' I smiled foreseeing the time ahead.

'Well, Bhai Jaan must be reaching in few minutes. Let's plan out the day ahead.' She commanded. Unaware of their pre determined plan, I felt to be the follower and the girl taking the lead. The picture was usually different in Indian society, particularly in these small towns.

Siddhartha was yet another sheep who was now seen in the scene. The group finally closed it on to 'JITENDRA TALKIES' for the matinee show of 'SOLDIER'. During All these times my sentiments were put to simmer to get it even more condensed. I was just looking to mask her with them.

We straightway moved towards the theatre. Balcony tickets were purchased from the counter and we still had about forty five minutes to spare. I had no urge to waste time in a group talk and preferred to sit as couples under the nearby tree.

I wanted to start with my glazed emotions by then, but I wondered how? Saying 'I LOVE YOU' daily was now boring and I lacked the skills to create a romantic situation with mere words. I finally initiated holding her hands and looking into her eyes, and ended up making the situation hold gravity. I wish I could spread my arms and hold her within me which could spell my emotions out.

'Ruchi'. My soft voice curved her neck towards me.

'I am sorry. Actually I have hidden about me to you. I want to confess it now.' My head went down as if I was confessing rape.

'What?' A shocked, tensed and incomplete voice from Ruchi questioned me.

I proceeded after a small silence. 'I am epileptic. Yes, I feel you know about the neuro problem.'

She looked tensed. May be she was figuring out the possible casualties that could happen to me. I was also tensed due to the outcome of this reality.

And before some more words were exchanged, Jaya came as usual with her cheeky smile, quite oblivion of the situation. She pulled me away and whispered in my ears, 'At least show some physical intimacy when you are with her alone. A girl feels otherwise if you don't…'

I smiled with shyness and nodded to abide by her advice. But the situation did not advise me to follow that. We went inside the almost vacant theatre and sat beside Ruchi. I had no clue where Jaya and Sid were. They had an old habit to disappear.

The movie started but I was continuously staring Ruchi by the side. She holds my hands this time and looked at me.

'Epilepsy is a neurological disorder which is caused by…………. It is characterized by unusual unconsciousness and fits……. It can be cured with regular doses of Sodium ions in the form of ……………' She told me more than what I knew about Epilepsy.'

She smiled and continued, 'I know you are epileptic, so what. Leena told me this once in the beginning. But I am sorry that you thought I would change my mind hearing the same. I love you and nothing can deter me from that.' She ended with tears rolling down her cheeks.

I wiped them with my fingers and put her head on my shoulder after I kissed her on the forehead. Thanks to the Bollywood movies that I had learnt to deal with those situations. I could do nothing more to what Jaya advised as I failed to understand the degree of intimacy she spoke of.

We came out of the theatre and all during the film we were busy gossiping. I wished they had the provision to pay only for the seats and not for the screen. It was almost evening and Siddhartha hurried to return back.

We went straight to the Bus stand. Ruchi got down on the way and went to her room. She told us to wait in the bus stand. She came with a packet and gave it to me. Yet another gift, but this time she showed it to me. It was a navy blue stone wash shirt, similar to what she had.

'Tell everybody that Sharan Bhaiya had gifted. It will be easy' she suggested. This girl had all the talent to be in some intelligence bureau, I wondered.

Similar things happened with Siddhartha as wel and we left for Dhanbad once again.

Reaching home I demonstrated the shirt by walking a ramp in my drawing room. Everybody was too innocent to believe that the Shirt was gifted to me by Sharan Bhaiya. My rapport in house also needs to be given credit.

'See how quickly people start loving Aniruddha.' My chachi concluded. She was wrong there, but right as well. I folded the shirt and put it inside the almirah with an extra care.

I didn't call the girls reaching home and I was waiting for the next morning and finally retired to the sofa cum bed in the night after a little study.

Bhai Kaka had actually employed a guy to manage the PCO as he was getting more into politics now. Yet I went to the PCO after breakfast in the morning to relieve *Bhai Kaka* till the boy comes. *Bhai Kaka* was delighted as he was going to his in law's place and so was I, though I was not going to mine. The species called '*in laws*' are special.................................

Ruchi's call was right thrree. Each time I spoke to her over the phone, I repeated the same old things like future, career, love etc taking both of us into account. This time I detailed her about how I managed with her gift last evening. A usual 'I love you' was well suffixed.

I returned home as soon as the boy came, and went straight inside Bhai Kaka's room to meet my young twin cousins. Bhai Kaka was around.

'Bring me your shirt you brought yesterday.' He said in a normal tone. My face distorted as if someone had asked me to share one of my Kidneys.

'Why that. I mean it's not that great.' I said trying to de motivate Bhai Kaka's wish.

'I need the blue colour and that's perfect.'

'Fine, I will give you another blue. It's Raymonds'. This time I wanted to woo him with the brand fame.

'No. I want that one only.' He insisted like a kindergarten kid for a lollypop. His stubborn was rigid. Why the hell he needs to go to in laws place when his wife is here; I said to myself.

'But why are you so possessive about this shirt? You were never so earlier.'

'Just because it is still new. I have not yet used once and this is a gift to me.' I said in a shaken voice which strengthened later.

'Fine, wear the shirt and come back from market in 15 minutes. That will solve your problem.' It was a check-mate situation. I was trapped.

Unable to design a better reply I shot, 'I won't give this to anybody. Please.' My body language illustrated my unhappiness.

My chachi smiled with her tightened lip. It was not a joke from any angle, I wondered.

'Okay, don't give the shirt, but I will say one thing.' Bhai kaka speaks in a reserved tone as he selects a shirt from his wardrobe.

'What' I said low, with sense of guilt.

'Your Sharan Bhaiya sounds feminine.'

'Just because you didn't get the shirt.'

'Because I heard both of yours detailed discussion now in the parallel line. It was nice' He smiled at me and turned to chachi.

'That was Ruchi right. Her voice is very sweet.' Chachi this time as if they had a gadget to measure sweetness.

I took a spontaneous 'about turn' and fled from the scene. Far from their sight I was praising Bhai kaka's ability to act. I had heard that he used to act the role of *NARAD MUNI* in local stage dramas.

Though there was a tension associated with what happened but it cooled myself as the drama ended with smiles in my uncle's face.

I shared this with Ruchi later, only to be blamed. I finally assured her that it did not get any voltage in my house.

THE FLAVOURS OF LOVE

*I*n few days Ruchi was back in Dhanbad as wel. The telecommunication was discontinued as she did not have a telephone at her house. Though the colliery where her father worked gave him a phone, it was for use within the colliery numbers. Nevertheless outsiders could call there with an extension number, it was risky on our part as the telephone operator of the office interviewed the caller upto the place of birth.

Ruchi managed to call me only if she was away from home. It was rarely possible as the exams were approaching fast.

The first to go was CBSE-PMT. It was the main focus as it had the maximum number of seat. The nearest centre was Calcutta. In the early hours of Saturday I reached Dhanbad Railway station.

Though the station looks gigantic with hundreds of Ambassador Cars in the entrance, yet a station is a station, particularly in India. I moved inside splitting the spitting crowd to get an early access to the train, I saw Ruchi on the over bridge with her father.

I tried to call her but I remembered that Ruchi had warned me not to do any such thing in front of her father. He resembled *Kroorsingh* or so due to his ideologies. Girl's fathers are anyways like that only as portrayed in movies at least.

My little intelligence advised me to vocalize my name to get Ruchi's attention only, without disturbing her father's concentration to move up the bridge.

'Aniruddha......Aniruddha .... I shouted keeping an eye on Ruchi. She turned and we exchanged smiles though she gestured me to maintain distance.

Following them up to their compartment in the Coal Field Express, I could see them entering the compartment and settling in. I did that against Ruchi's choice only to find that it was a ladies compartment.

But Ruchi's dad was a gentleman. Even if not gentle, yet he was man and so he lost all the rights to travel in that compartment. I entered to find few other mid forty type men in the swarm of pretty girls. Fathers were allowed for that day, I guessed. A plump lady in Railway Protection Police Force attire was there to guard the beauties. Her *gulab jamun* type round eyes rolled over me. I quickly realized that I was in a wrong place.

'Ae', she called as she moved towards me. 'This is ladies compartment. Can't u see?' She completed in an obvious police tone. She lacked the feminism in her voice as well.

'Yes didi, actually..........' I tried to emotionally capture her calling her so but she was not moved.

'Can you please allow me here? Other compartments are too full & I will stand near the doors only.' I pleaded her as if she was Ruchi's mother and I wanted to marry her daughter. My timid expressions melted the soft heart inside her tough build as she nodded in affirmation with a short smile.

'Come inside a little. Don't stand near the gate. It's risky.' She said as I wondered as how people change their stances with few nice words. The world needs peace and love, I concluded, and I was in the right track.

I bought two tetra packs of Frooti and shared it with the lady. She protested thinking it to be a bribe but settled as I tried to be over affectionate. She took it and placed in her bag as I sipped one with short glimpses over Ruchi.

The train set off with a long siren as all the girls immersed themselves in their books. Ruchi was trapped in the text materials of Brilliant Tutorials in the last window seat adjacent to the door. I could see all the sentences were underlined with a red ink. It looked more like an examination sheet of a failed candidate. I wondered the use of underlining if everything in the book was important.

I drifted myself little inside to shift the load of my bag from the shoulder to the wooden shelves. As I turned, I collided head-On with Mr. Kroorsingh.

'I am sorry. Excuse me please.' I said pretending to be unknown. I expected him to have a short memory and would have forgotten my face.

He reply was a continuous stare at my face concluding in a smile.

'Can't you hear, Excuse me' I yelled. I never knew from where did I got the balls to say so, or was it in panic. May be my closeness with the interim Railway Minister few minutes back fuelled these approach.

Not many people moved but Ruchi. She gestured unhappiness but the blunder was done. I could not signal her as my would-be father in law was still staring at me. Now he was concentrating on my eyes under the specs and with a bigger smile. I was in doubt if he ends it up proposing his love for me. I could never visualize this in wildest of my dreams.

'Beta, didn't you recognize me?' he asked affectionately. I thanked god that he did not go extremes. I looked at Ruchi from the corner of my eye. She was relaxed than earlier. I winked my eyes, still pretending to be unknown.

'You studied with Ruchi na..... at Bokaro.' He completed.

Artificial body language showing repentance covered my face like a make-up. 'I am really sorry uncle. Actually I could not recognize you due to the tensions of exam. Sorry.' I repeated.

'No issues. Take it easy'

'Where is Ruchi?' I exclaimed.

He turned towards the window to point towards her. Ruchi smiled but settled in a 'Hi' only. She wanted to reveal a casual friendship perhaps.

He began chatting with me some irrelevant topics. He started with Coal India Limited but I had limited knowledge of the same. The only thing I knew about coal was that it contains carbon and Anthracite is the best variety of coal. I wished he would ask me about my future plans and all those things that could make him feel that I am the perfect guy for his daughter. He didn't even ask my surname.

I was freed only when he found few others working in collieries to discuss issues like bonus, and trade unions.

Placing myself in a suitable condition I stared at Ruchi throughout the journey till we reached Calcutta. We diversified ourselves at the Howrah station to our respective lodging places.

My Bengali knowledge helped me in my travel in the city. I was right there well before time at the examination centre the next day. None of the faces were familiar as I browsed through them.

Thinking of touching my mother's feet, I closed my eyes and concentrated on them. It was more a belief and respect than customary. I kissed the hall ticket when Ruchi slipped into my mind. It was the ticket to Ruchi.

I was somewhere pleased to see the question paper. Managing to answer 132 out of the 200 questions, I had developed the sight to make it there.

I was happy but I could not trace Ruchi on my way back to Dhanbad. Quite possible they returned in a different train or a reserved compartment this time.

'Yes, it was nice. I solved around 130. How many you did?' Ruchi questioned. She called from a PCO as Jaya took her out from the confinement of her house, a couple of days after the exams.

'Me too around the same.'

'But what were you doing with my father! Pagal Ho?' Thank God, he is little impressed with you.'

'But how?'

'Even I am Shocked.'

'Ruchi, I am feeling like to meet you'

'Not possible. Somehow Jaya managed to get me out today. Minu is with us only. You better concentrate for AIIMS. Perhaps I will not be able to speak for all these days.'

'How can you be so cruel?'

'It's not like that. Even I miss you. And hello… I love you as well.'

'I love you too.' I said to end the call, which I wished to long for hours at least. My voice was loud enough for my Chachi to hear in the kitchen. Thankfully dadi was not around.

She came out exited with the oil coated steel spatula and smiled. 'Who….Sharan Bhaiya?'

I smiled blushingly. ' Please don't tell to anybody.' I pleaded.

'Fine, but study hard if you really want to get her…..' She said as she ran towards the kitchen smelling something burning.

❅ ❅ ❅

Several entrance examinations were on the cards but I was more than eager for the AIIMS. Not that because it was the premium medical college of the country, but for the fact that both me and Ruchi shared the same examination centre.

Few more examinations were over and we had no clues of each other's performances.

I was all set to leave for Calcutta a day ahead for my exams. I woke up early in the morning and went to the bathroom to bathe. I could dare that just because it was summer.

'Aaaaaaaaaaaaaaaaaaaaaaaaaaaaa.' Terrible sound echoed from the bathroom followed by some breaking noise.

Dadi's alert ears captured them in the almost silent

surrounding. She followed the sound to the bathroom to check but could do nothing as the door was bolted from inside.

'Ani'... 'Ani', she screamed my nick name repeatedly. *Bhai kaka* ran towards the Bathroom. Everyone knew what had actually happened, as this happened once previously as wel, around a year back.

Bhai kaka slammed the door but could not manage to open it. He desperately opened the toilet door and sneaked inside the bathroom from a slim gap of the median. He opened the door from inside. I was still senseless with little froth around my lips. The bucket had already broken, unable to withstand the pressure of my body when I fell on it, resulting in cuts and bruises all around. My body cordoned the perimeter of the small cubicle of the bathroom like a dead snake.

Bhai Kaka and chachi did their best to lift my carcass off to the living room. I was laid on the floor over a mattress, with *dadi* fanning me with a traditional palm leaf fan along with the speeding ceiling fan over my face.

Soon I started gaining my consciousness. I could see my close ones with worried faces. *Bhai kaka* sobbed hiding his face; the most emotional of the lot. I tried to recapitulate in the midst of huge headache and hangover about the incident, but I could remember that I went to take bath and nothing more.

In few hours my parents were there. The headache had also somewhat subdued. I was still eager to go to Calcutta for obvious reasons, but none supported my idea.

'Fifty seats in all, twenty of which is reserved. No point in going for it after this.' *Mejo Kaka* (another uncle) claimed. He was the most *darpok* of my family.

'You are just getting extra scary' I replied.

'I am not *darpok,* just that a little practical. And you concentrate on your medicines. It can't happen unless you skip them.' He was really torturing me when I was expecting some soft words after all that. I wished Ruchi to be around.

A lot of efforts and emotional drama were put to practice to convince them. My career, my life.....and many more. I was allowed to go by the evening train with my mother.

We reached Calcutta by the night and preferred hotel than relatives for the night. 'At least you can revise the last time there and why to take un-necessary obligations if hotels are available.'

My mother's formal approach to our far relatives won over mine. I however found it better to save some grands and use it otherwise, may be for buying some gifts for Ruchi.

'*Maa* fast. We will get late.' I said irritated. May be my father's inference to all the theories regarding to ladies owes its base here.

'Okay, it's done. You have stopped praying to gods, not even in exams.' She said putting her flat sandals. I smiled at her thought as if god sets the papers or he will check it.

'I have asked god for something. Let me see if he helps me out there.'

'What?'

'I will tell you in some time.'

'If you try to do something from the core of your heart, destiny takes care of the rest.' She said thoughtfully.

'I smiled again as I knew how truly I want that and is trying for that.'

We reached the examination centre at Alipore well before time. Puzzled faces were around and this time the crowd was more sincere type. May be the lesser number of seats had prompted only the book worms to brawl in the rat race. I checked for Ruchi before anything but could not find her. My mother also scanned the girls as if she was there to find a bride for me.

I could see series of taxis painted in yellow and black arriving with the potential doctors. Ruchi came out from one of them, parked at a little far away from where we stood. She was in a white *salwar kameez* and was shining bright. Her father was there as well with a slim lady and a cute little girl; her mother and sister probably. I could guess only as I had never met them. Ruchi led the family with confident steps as if she was the flag bearer in a sporting event.

I turned my face avoiding eye contact with Ruchi and particularly her father. Scared to talk to Ruchi because of the parents around, and to kroorsingh because of his Coal India discussions.

'Are Ruchi tum.' My mother caught hold of her hand as she passed by. She knew her from the days my mother used to visit Leena at Bokaro. Ruchi was shocked, so was I.

Her parents followed. 'Namaste Aunty.' She said and turned towards her mother.

'Aunty this is my mummy, and Mummy she is Aunty....I mean Leena's cousin brother's mother. Perhaps this was the safest way to introduce she could design to hide even a slight hint of our relationship.

Both the ladies smiled at each other with the formal '*Namaste*'. My mother turned to kroorsingh to greet him as well. He just smiled in acknowledgement.

Sensing a suitable time , I evolved from nowhere. 'Maa, where are you?' I appeared to be skeptical.

'Beta see, Ruchi with her mother. Say Namaste.' She directed to me as if I was a three year old kid. I wonder as to whether whom I should say 'Namaste', only Ruchi's mother or Ruchi as wel, or may be her sister too. I was always scared of these protocols. Thankfully Ruchi's father had walked few yards ahead as I could see him around a pack of beautiful Bengali aunties.

'Come, let's sit. It is still thirty five minutes to get inside' I said and guided them to a domesticated grass lawn. I decided to start discussing things with Ruchi, but failed as her father signaled towards me, '*Babu jara idhar aana.*'

I looked at Ruchi but she smiled at my situation. I leaped towards kroorsingh and said 'Namaste' to him.

He smiled and walked away. I followed him up to a paan

kiosk. He took few *paan* with *zarda* and *tulsi* and bought few Eclairs. He took few bottles of Bisleri as well.

'Take these for all of you' he said 'Anything else you want for you' He completed.

'No thanks uncle.' I said as I kept the answer reserved for future. I returned back and distributed the Eclairs among Ruchi and Minu. I took one as well. Minu was happy having more chocolates than Ruchi and she smiled. She went to her mother's lap and teased Ruchi for not letting her sit there.

'Come and sit here beta.' My mother pulled Ruchi on her lap. I was guessing the reason of my mother being over affectionate to Ruchi, may be some telepathy or so. I still wondered if Kroorsingh would come and ask me to sit on his shoulders and would ferry me across Alipore.

'Your name is Aniruddha na, you topped in the coaching right?' Ruchi's mother spoke to me for the first time. I smiled in affirmation and blushed simultaneously.

'Ruchi is also good at studies, I know.' My mother said without any supportive ideas. 'She also makes good tea. My husband is so fond of her tea that now every time I make tea, he says it's nice but not like what Ruchi makes.' She flattered.

Both the mothers were soon engrossed in usual ladies discussions. They looked similar and their nature was matching as well. They discussed everything from sarees, to cuisines to daily soaps. I had a little liberty to speak to my darling and we discussed few important chapters. Minu was somewhere busy with her éclairs.

'It would be great if both of them are selected in AIIMS.' Ruchi's mother said as she pointed towards me and Ruchi.

'Yes, at least they would go and come together.' *Maa* said, still giving importance to petit issues than studies. I gave an irritated look to my mother to stop her from speaking something irrelevant.

The final bell rang and now the candidates were allowed to enter the examination centre.

I started with touching my mother's feet and just as I stood up my mother signaled towards Ruchi's mother and said, 'And aunty.'

I had no other options left than to touch her feet as well. Thank god Kroorsingh was not around.

My obedience compelled Ruchi to follow what I did. My mother kissed both of ours forehead. I was shocked to see her doing this. She never did this earlier.

'Where is *Papa*?' Ruchi enquired as her eyes rotated all around.

I almost laughed thinking of the answer, but I controlled somehow. 'He must be taking a stroll around the area.' I faked.

' *Koi baat nahin beta*, you go or you will be late.' Ruchi's mother said convincingly.

We entered separately and held each other's hand as soon as we were out of our parent's sight.

'I bet by the time we will come out of the examination centre, our mothers will even decide whether our children would select Engineering or Medical' I said.

She smiled. 'But it's good na that our parents met each other.'

'Of course yes, and most importantly they liked each other's company as well. I don't think we will have many difficulties convincing them once we are through with the medicals.'

We felt like being in the sea beach and not for AIIMS entrance examination.

The test started and ended in no time. I selected the best alternative answers out of every four; more with a gut feel than any reasons behind them. Perhaps I felt that touching feet of two mothers will do the needful.

I came out of the examination hall smiling. Ruchi was already there. 'How many you solved?' she exclaimed.

'Around 90%. And you.' I replied.

'Similar, but people say that the cut off goes to somewhere around 95%. Let's see what happens.' She put figures to state that the exam was good but not great. Everyone listened to us like reporters in a press conference.

'Okay, we will leave for the station now. We have our train in another couple of hours.' My mother said to Ruchi's mother. Their hearts were glued together by Fevicol by then.

'*Beta, kabhi apni maa ko lekar hamare ghar aao.*' Aunty said and Kroorsingh came in chorus.

'Yes aunty, certainly.' I said. How could I kill the first invitation to my girlfriend's house, that too by her parents?

✳ ✳ ✳

We reached home safely. Only one examination was left- BCECE- the entrance examination for medical colleges in Bihar. We had a gap of about a month and tried level best to remain in the study mode.

Calling her over phone had been comparatively easier, though I was scared of the telephone operator who used to forward the calls to her house from Kroorsingh's office. 'She might hear our talks.' Ruchi once said me, I remember.

CBSE-PMT results were out by then. None of us including Leena and Jaya could get through. I could hear Ruchi cry over the phone but could not consulate her. Neither was I equipped with ideas, nor was even I in a state to do so. For me no Medicals had only one synonym, which was- 'Forget Ruchi'.

Leena's mother lived nearby. She was there at our house that day.

'This result was pre declared. It was bound to happen. They never went there to study but doing stupid things. Those girls there....... Forget it.' Her expressions showed her hatred for these girls. It was like blaming the opposition after losing the elections.

Situation was turning grave. I wanted to meet Ruchi at any

cost and shared my feelings with her. Of course I had a way out. A visit to her place could do it for me. Ruchi suggested me to come with a book, the reason for me being there.

Sharp at nine at left my house for her's. It was a 30 minutes travel by shared Auto. I moved inside a colony at Dhansar as guided by Ruchi but could not find their house in the first half an hour.

I could manage their quarter only after consulting a paan kiosk. Of course he knew the address of his regular customer.

I opened the gate and moved inside, crossing the garden at the onset. 'Mr. R.S.P Singh' was written quite bold. Recapitulating the full name I wondered how his teacher would have managed while taking roll calls. 'Ravi............ Shankar.......... Prasad.......... Singh!!!!!!!!!!!!!!Yes Ma'am. Quite possible two or three students to reply on the same name as well.

Soon my eyes concentrated on a dark metallic board with some Urdu verse engraved on it. I wondered I have landed at a wrong place, but I had knocked the door by then.

The door opened almost instantly as if someone was just kept in duty for that purpose. It was Ruchi's mother. I had a sigh of relief.

'What Happened?'

'No, actually I was wondering about this board in Urdu.' I replied.

'Your uncle's friend has gifted it. Says, it brings good luck.' She described. 'Come in.' She added.

I could see Ruchi adjusting her skirt getting down of her bed. It was a stereotype 3 BHK quarter as we also had. A nice 21 inches color TV was placed on the top of a stand custom made for that purpose only. A movable air cooler was positioned at an angle to cater to all the persons sitting in the living room. The honey colored sofa set suited well with the walls distempered with a cheddar cheese shade.

'Sit na, why are you standing.' Ruchi's mother said pointing towards the couch. 'Ruchi beta, where are you? See Aniruddha has come.' Her pitch was louder this time.

I felt like falling into quick sand as I tried to sit on the couch. I was almost one foot deep and my pelvic bone was well submerged within.

'How is your mother? She asked.

'She is fine.' I said and rotated my neck to see the artifacts hung around. Though I knew Kroorsingh had a great taste there at AIIMS exams in Calcutta only, yet a nice portrait of 'MONALISA' diagonally opposite to where I was seated confirmed the fact.

Aunty went inside the kitchen and soon came out with chilled water and Rasna on a tray. I preferred water feeling that choosing Rasna is against etiquette. But I could not control and emptied the glass tumbler having Rasna in the next minute as soon as Aunty went back to kitchen.

Ruchi came to the living room and sat beside me on the couch. She was surely busy with comb and lip gloss during all these times, is what I could make out seeing her face.

Unable to be in command of my emotions, I planted a kiss on her cheek. Her eyes moved towards the open window and mine towards the kitchen.

'Pagal ho?' she whispered.

'Where is Minu?' I smiled and diverted her from the question.

'School.' She replied.

'And Papa....I mean yours?'

'He has gone to office, but you ask about me. You are here to meet me, right?' She said irritated and in a jealous tone.

'I am here to study madam.' I said smiling to add a sense of pun to it. Her elbow thrashed me as a punishment for the same.

Aunty returned back with yet another platter. This time it was Paneer Pakoda. ' Beta try these Pakodas. They are your uncle's favorite dish. He always likes them golden brown; crispy and spicy from outside but soft and juicy from inside.' I wondered whether he wanted a pakoda or a porn star.

I took one Pakoda and placed it into my mouth. Really delicious it was. 'Do you also know to cook such palatable Pakodas?' I questioned towards Ruchi.

'I can only make tea and it tastes very good, ask your father if you want.' She boasted.

'How are your preparations for the Bihar Medicals going on?' Aunty asked me straightaway.

'Fine...' but before I could complete Ruchi intervened. 'I wanted to discuss few Physics numerical with you.' I took the paneer pakoda platter and followed Ruchi to her room. Aunty was back in kitchen.

We started with some physics numerical but concluded that the acceleration due to gravity of earth was less than the attraction in her eyes. I was lost in them like a comet in the black hole of universe.

'Ruchi, have you ever thought what if we can't make it to the medicals? What if we can't impress each other's family?' I asked in a worried tone. I held her hand as our fingers entangled with each other.

'We will elope' She said very casually. 'I remember one of my relatives eloped with a Bengali. He was Biswas. Initially there were repercussion but everyone accepted them later.' She described quite confidently.

'I don't want that. I want my whole clan to celebrate our wedding. I want your father to hand over your hand to me.' I sounded concerned.

'Don't worry; we will surely make out some way. Anyways I am still in dilemma about your family's regional origin. You are actually a Bengali or Bihari?

'We are actually Kanyakubz Bramhins from Kannauj but now have learnt the local and Bengali culture after we have migrated here' I said as I described her all about my forefather's marriage stories.

'If g = 9.8 m/s square, then MANGO IS CALLED MANGIFERA

INDICA' She said and quickly removed her hands out of mine. Her face was also suddenly terrified.

'What? But how can you relate both of these?' I was shocked to hear that she had somehow managed to get Newton and Aristottle married.

She peeped out of her room and sighed relief. 'I felt like mummy arrived.' She said. We sat together again with interlocked fingers.

Unexpectedly her mother arrived. It was real this time. Ruchi held my hand even tighter and uses the second hand as well. 'No it's not fever.' She announced. Her confidence was actually more than what is generally seen in a doctor.

'What happened?' Aunty worriedly asked. The mother was actually disguised by the acting skills of the daughter.

'He is not feeling good mummy.' Ruchi explained.

'Might be due to some acidity problem? Did you have your breakfast today? Generally it happens due to an empty stomach. Is there any headache? Wait, let me bring some cold milk.' Aunty asked a series of questions without letting me answer any. I wondered if she'd also tried for those medical entrance examinations.

'Cold milk! How can I? I mean I can manage the hot milk somehow, but I don't like cold milk at all.' I protested to Ruchi.

'Happiness comes at a price dear.' She smiled sarcastically as she said so.

Aunty was swift enough to bring a glass full of cold milk along with the tablet of Gelusil MPS. 'Lo beta.' She insisted.

'Why are you calling him "*beta*"; is he your *beta*?' Ruchi charged at her mother as if she had committed the biggest fraud ever.

'So what, he is like my beta only.' Aunty replied calmly.

'No, you won't call him so.' Ruchi's voice still over-pitched.

'Okay Baba.' Aunty said and went back to the kitchen.

'Why the hell you were fighting with your mother. She is so caring and so good' I said, as I tried to show my disappointment.

'If you are her *beta* and I am her *beti*(daughter) then how are we related? I can't digest that.' She explained.

I could do nothing except smile at her stupid logic.

'Let me show you my parent's marriage album.' Ruchi insisted. I had no choice left when any such demand comes from her side.

As I opened the first page of the album, I could see my would-be mother-in-law in a *'Sadhna cut'* hair style and Bell Bottom outfits. Kroor Singh was also not far behind dense and long ear locks, depicting the look of a Bollywood 70's hero.

'Love marriage' I inquired flummoxed by their outfits.

'No!' she replied instantly. Her face changed red as if it were a crime if her parents did that, and was something marvelous if we were planning for it. She kept introducing me to everybody in the album and also grilled me regarding the processes in their marriage. Though it was immaterial for me unless the results were declared, yet I had to follow her.

By the time I reached the last page of the album, I had replaced Kroor Singh with me and Aunty by Ruchi. I was happy seeing both of us happily married.

I returned back home with the sun still far above the horizon. A sense of happiness and satisfaction easily reflected on my spindle-shaped face. Everybody believed that I had been to Siddhartha's house to discuss few physics problems.

TOSS THE CAREER
DELHI

'**W**hen they could not make it through to the CBSE Medicals, how can you expect them to crack other exams having very limited seats?' I could hear Leena's mother discussing it with *Maa* and *dadi*.

She was perhaps right this time. Anxiety surfaced on everybody's face with the results being announced gradually. Every dream of ours had its base there itself. The process finally ended with the announcement of the Bihar Medical's result. None of us qualified in either of the exams. Everyone was depressed in their own style.

Jaya decided to give it yet another shot. So did Ruchi. They might have felt that they had missed it by a fraction. Siddhartha got through Engineering in Bangalore. 'Everybody gets a chance there; plenty of colleges have mushroomed up.' People said so, or maybe it was a cover-up for the losers.

Leena too made her way towards the Engineering College in Karnataka- B I E T, Davangere pursuing Textile Engineering.

I had real doubts regarding my abilities. Every step of mine would be linked to the fate of others too.

I tried going to Patna for graduation but I was taken aback

seeing the standards there. I turned back to Manu for suggestion. He knew me in and out.

'You come to Delhi and get yourself admitted here. Complete your graduation and then apply for MBA. Your abilities suit this profession.' He everthing about MBA to me, about which I felt like a frog in a well.

Our discussion did last for around twenty five minutes and the STD pulse had beeped almost hundred times.

It was a tough job for me to persuade the entire family for this venture. I got irritated at times as to why all the family members had to do a round table conference when it came to taking any decisions related to me. Perhaps they all loved me a lot or they had no faith on my decision-making skills. I wondered what they would do when I would put forth my wish to marry Ruchi.

And to convince Ruchi was tougher. 'Delhi means no Medicals, and without getting into medicals how would you propose our marriage to everybody.' She screamed over the phone.

'I would make it to MBA and then……'

'It will take three years at least.' She said interrupting me in between.

'But what if I don't make it to Medicals this year as well?'

The debate ended in an emotional drama with Ruchi's voice trembling. 'I have faith in you. You will make things right.' She said

'I love you dear and I can't live without you.' I said to boost her.

'I love you too,' echoed in my ears for the next couple of hours.

Ticket was booked for Delhi and I was all set to leave on the 29th of August. Meeting Ruchi once before that was a must. Jaya arranged for the meet at her house.

Jaya's house was a three storied building situated at the heart of the city. I had a lot of apprehensions getting inside, but meeting Ruchi was sufficient enough reason to compensate all inhibitions. The hospitality bestowed was more than expected from the little upper strata of the society.

As I was escorted inside Jaya's room, I was happy to see Ruchi there. The room was lavishly decorated as seen in the movies. Maybe they had hired some interior designer for that purpose, Curtains with cascades and blinds and many more designing which I had never seen earlier. Jaya joined us soon after.

Jaya asked me various questions related to Delhi, my journey plans and the college. Ruchi did not utter a single word. I found her busy with a FILMFARE magazine featuring HRITIK ROSHAN.

As I answered to Jaya's queries, I also gestured her about Ruchi's mood. Her smile in reply gave me some confidence. Jaya left the room calling someone. I was guessing whether it was a courtesy on her part to give us few minutes of privacy or something else.

I moved towards Ruchi and sat beside her. 'Gussa Ho?' I whispered.

'Why should I?' She replied instantly. Girls generally require a lot of buttering for anything. I took her palm and placed it on mine, trying to snatch away the magazine.

'Don't.'

I wondered whether it was for the magazine or for her hand.

'Hritik is handsome but not as me.' I said laughingly, expecting her to advocate upon my stupid comments at least.

'When you can chant praises for Ameesha Patel day and night, why can't I praise Hritik?' I could identify her reason for being so infuriated.

I smiled at her juvenile nature and drew her closer to me and planted a kiss on her cheek. Action speaks louder than words, I believe. Her eyes became wet as she responded with similar passion.

A knock on the door drew us apart. Jaya came in with a tray

full of Bengali Sweets. Tea followed. Ruchi had wiped her tears by then.

I took a Rasgulla and placed it in Ruchi's mouth squeezing the sugar syrup out of it. She took a bite and placed the remaining in my mouth. I smiled with embarrassment as my tongue tasted the sweetness of the Rasgulla. It tasted even sweeter than the original one.

'Take care of yourself there. I've heard that the Delhi girls woo boys easily.' She said worried.

Conversations detailed into various topics and suggestions and a series of instructions followed. Some of them were even tougher than the preparation instructions for Mayonnaise.

'How good would it have been, if you could have accompanied me to Delhi!' I said as I also visualized both of us in the RAC seat of the sleeper class in the Kalka mail. Ruchi smiled at my wish as if it was too big to be granted. Jaya changed the mood between us with various topics.

The big wall clock hanging on the wall rang twelve times indicating it was noon. It was the only primitive article in the otherwise modern room of Jaya's.

"However close you are to someone, yet you can't enjoy their companionship at all times; particularly when you need to hug your girlfriend for the first time."

Jaya was quick to understand this. 'Wait, let me get some water for you' she said as she walked out of the room.

Wasting no time I enveloped Ruchi into my arms. Though impulsive, I wanted us to be like that throughout my life.

Both Ruchi and Jaya came down to see me off. The moment of separation always makes the heart heavy. Ruchi sobbed within and I resisted the tears to come out. I boarded an auto and moved. I could see Ruchi from the speeding auto, standing and gazing at me, getting drenched in the rain.

Regular calls were made from both ends until the day of departure arrived.

There was yet another pile of instructions. This time it came from my parents and guardians. Even the kids at home did not stay behind. 'Don't eat anything given by strangers.' My mother said.

Don't stand near the gates; don't get down at different platforms; and many more directives followed from all corners of my house. 'Most importantly don't forget to take medicines' my father said.

'*Bhaiya*, you must visit Red Fort, India Gate and Rashtrapati Bhavan. They are tourist spots in Delhi. I have read about them in my General knowledge book.' One of my cousin brothers suggested. Everybody did their best of research-work to give me an idea to settle in a new city altogether.

My mother and aunts had prepared some *Gujiyas, Nimki* and *nariyal Laddoos* for me to take them to Delhi. 'Take these and give to your friends as well.' My mother said. I guess they did not assume how selfish I was.

I left for Delhi solely on Manu's assurance. I otherwise had no idea of where I was going to stay, which college I would get admitted to and select which subjects as well.

I reached the Dhanbad railway station at 10 pm. I was bound to board the Kalka mail at 11.pm. It was the first time in my life that I was travelling for such a long distance all alone.

I was excited about going to Delhi but I had started missing Ruchi already. Hawkers, vendors, porters all seemed to resemble her. Earlier I thought that these things were just the creative ideas of the screenplay writers in movies. But I was wrong.

I walked down the platform up to the end where there was a cafeteria. It had been a meeting spot for both of us in the past. Thousands of thoughts cruised in my mind together, some good some bad, fighting with each other. 'Will I be able to make Ruchi mine' was the crucial question.

That bud of a red Rose, sharing sips of tea in those chipped China cups of the Cafeteria and making her angry by speaking ill about Kroor Singh... All took me to a different world altogether. I never knew that the train was in the platform by then.

Hurriedly I bumped inside another bogie as the train was about to leave. By the time I reached my assigned berth, the train had almost crossed two stations. There was someone else resting on my berth.

'Excuse me, this is my seat.' I claimed.

'But the TTE has allotted me this.' He replied.

'But how can he? I have a valid ticket.' I said confidently, as confident as I was about my gender.

'Your boarding station is Dhanbad, why are you boarding at Koderma?' the TTE said as he intervened.

'It's not like that.' I told him what happened and put forward all possible logics to get my seat back. But the TTE was still reluctant to allot my seat back to me. He must have been bribed with some Gandhian currencies.

I yelled hysterically at him to retaliate with my vocal chords swollen. It got the co-passengers to wake up and at last the TTE surrendered.

I went up to the upper berth allotted to me and took out Ruchi's 4*6 inches photograph. I completed a conversation with Ruchi doing her share of communication as well. I did not know when I slept but woke up only during brunch as I saw the females of the Gujrati family in my compartment offering Poories and Subji to the other members. 'Can I have one poori?' emerged from somewhere within my body but subsided before coming out of mouth.

Several stations passed. All were similar if the yellow and Black board was removed. The chaiwala told me it was Mughalsarai. 'This is the biggest station in the chord line like Jollarpettai in the South. The trains change their engine and hence they halt for about half an hour here.' One co passenger educated me with the details.

I thought of coming down the train and calling Ruchi from a PCO. There was a huge queue. As I got my turn, I dialed Ruchi's number.

'Can you please connect it to extension 468' I requested.

The same old music played as I was kept on hold, making my heart to beat faster.

'Hello' I heard. Ruchi's voice it was.

But before I could respond my eyes fell on the accelerating train. Putting the cradle down I rushed towards the train. The PCO owner ran after me for money. He must have shouted slangs, but they did not reach my ears. I took out a five rupees coin out of my pocket and tossed it on him as I caught hold of the train.

This cheeky experience forced me to stay glued to my berth till I reached Delhi at around 7.30 pm. It was Purani Dilli.

I came out of into the platform of a densely populated station. Everything was same like Geeta Press Book Stall, Railway Catering Contractor's Shop, and the crowd with a little different accent of Hindi than what I heard it in Dhanbad. It was tough to make it out that I was in the country's capital being there in the station.

My eyes browsed through almost every one of them until the train departed and the crowd settled. But I could not manage to see Manu and Thapa, who were supposed to receive me.

I looked for a PCO and went out of the station in the process. But before the PCO I could spot a board reading 'PRE PAID AUTO STAND'. It was a challenge for me to reach Manu and I accepted it without delay. In spite of calling Manu, I queued up to get a pre paid auto up to Delhi University.

'North campus, Kirori Mal College.' I said.

'Seventy five Rupees' the clerk said as he handed over the receipt to me.

I took the receipt and moved ahead towards the auto rickshaw. The autowalla's eyes inflated like a balloon and soon shrunk as if someone had punctured it. May be he was looking for a larger distance client, I thought.

He drove along the streets narrower than what I expected,

but soon I got the real picture of the capital city. I took my face out of the rickshaw, reading the names of the various areas I was passing by, Mukherjee Nagar, Mall Road being some of them. I was disguised by the name as I thought it to be some red light area.

'*Bhaiya, Ye mall road kaisa naam hua?*' I asked the rick guy unable to control my inquisitiveness.

He smiled as I could see in the rear view mirror, but he preferred not to answer. Perhaps he was still annoyed with me for travelling lesser distance.

I peeped out of the auto once again to read a blue board directing 'UNIVERSITY ENCLAVE'. My confidence boosted and satisfaction enhanced.

Passing all the colleges, the name of which I had learnt from Manu, I reached Kamala Nagar market.

'What happened?' I asked as the rick guy switched off the ignition.

'It's there.' He said as he pointed towards a big gate beside a United Colors of Benetton showroom.

'But why is the gate closed?' I asked surprised.

This is the back gate. You need to go around the college campus for the front gate. 'He suggested.

'So take me there.' I said with obvious expression.

'Your receipt says Kirori Mal College, the gate is not specified.' He tried to prove himself logically correct, or may be politically correct as per the city standards.

I took my luggage out, without bothering to give elasticity to the fight. The Rickshaw guy drove away fast, smiling. Perhaps he took revenge from me for not travelling long.

Dazed with the sight of beautiful girls and elegant shops, I somehow forgot where to go. Shortly my eyes fell on a guy who seemed to be from the North-east. It worked faster than a 'Quick Action Analgesic Pill'. Happily I leaped towards him and turned him around holding his shoulders.

My face changed instantly as if I had tasted Neem mistakenly for sugar. I managed a clumsy 'Sorry' somehow. It was a wrong assumption on my part that there would be only one person of Leel Bahadur Thapa type. Actually there were plenty.

Defeated by the situation I finally decided to call Manu and dialed his hostel's number from a nearby PCO.

'KMC boys hostel' the receiver confirmed.

'Can I speak to Kr. Amit Manu, room number 29' I said in a formal manner.

'Wait a minute please'

I waited with the phone on my ear as I heard the guy shouting 'Manu, phone call for you'. The pause ended when I heard a heavy Hello from the other side. I could easily recognize the voice. It was Avikal, Manu's elder brother.

'Hello Bhaiya, this is Aniruddha Trivedi. I am near the back gate of your college. How can I come from here?' I said with little hesitation.

'But where are Manu and Thapa? Okay, you just wait there; I will be there in few minutes.' He seized his enquiry halfway and suggested.

I narrated him the episode with Thapa's look alike as we entered the hostel gate laughing.

Manu and Thapa returned in sometime after unable to trace me at Purani Dilli Railway Station. Conventional hugging followed.

'We even got your name announced from the announcement desk.' Manu said.

'May be I left earlier and you reached later?'

Avikal Bhaiya left us alone to open our hearts better. We tuned in to a different frequency altogether.

'I am quite sure that you reached here in the process of following some chick. Isn't it?' Manu claimed; confident of my past records.

'No yaar, I have changed my point of view and approach for girls.' I said pretending to be sober.

'So you approach them from the front now.' Thapa said and laughed. Both of them left no stones unturned in pulling my leg.

I acquainted them with the script of my love story and I also showed them Ruchi's photograph. They could not believe in the transformation in me.

'*Trivedi, Trivedi nahi raha*', was now their latest slogan. We recalled stories from the past. Thapa and Manu had an infatuation in school. I was more of a rebellious leader of the class than being a lover boy. But equations had changed with times.

Both Thapa and Manu took me to introduce with their friends, Rahul and Sanket in particular. Rahul was a handsome guy from Ranchi but had a polio-infected leg. Sanket was however a plum-bodied lad from Dhanbad.

As we moved into Rahul and Sanket's room on the ground floor, they welcomed me like we were *chaddi* buddies.

'Shocked? They know about your *chaddi* size as well', Manu described. I searched for that perfect expression to fit in that situation.

We settled in on his bed, resting our spine against the wall. Manu supported me with a pillow, which I kept on my lap.

The exposed bosom of Jennifer Lopez in a big poster pasted on the wall and few Maxim magazines were sufficient for me to understand Rahul's art of living. Maybe I did not match pace with the world, but the Debonair magazines under the mattress supported my ideas.

Our discussions covered everything except 'what I was there for'. They kept on boasting about their college.

'Amitabh Bacchhan graduated from this college and used to stay in the same room in which Manu stays.' Sanket said proudly.

'Even Shah Rukh Khan studied his first year B Com here.' Thapa added.

Shahrukh Khan's name reminded me of Ruchi. He was her favorite actor. While they continued with college whereabouts, I had only physical presence there.

We returned back to Manu's room and I slept sandwiched between Manu and Thapa.

✻ ✻ ✻

My first morning in Delhi started with the breakfast in the room brought either by Manu or Thapa. By the time I woke up, they had already left for their classes. I was accompanied by Avikal Bhaiya.

'So, what are your plans?' Bhaiya asked.

'No……. I mean nothing as yet. Manu called me and I came. That's it.' I sounded like an idiot.

He smiled with an intended sarcasm. 'Well you discuss things with Manu and others and we will plan things for tomorrow.' He said and left me in solitude to fight with the depressing vibes.

An admission to Delhi University Colleges gets over by mid-July and it was September. I felt pity for myself being there two months after the admission dates and that too with a meager percentage of 63% aggregate, where the last cut off goes at 85%.

Whenever you are sad, you miss the person you are closest to, and in loneliness it multiplies. Ruchi's thoughts and memories did Salsa in front of my eyes. My eyes were fixed on the rotating fan that hung to the ceiling and my mind pre-occupied with my career woes.

A knock at the door busted my meditation. 'What's up man?' Thapa enquired in an energetic tone. Either he enjoyed his last class a lot or was happy to bunk the post lunch session; there was something that could be studied from his activities.

Manu carried some Aaloo Paranthas from the mess for me. I was otherwise an unauthorized immigrant dwelling there. Soon they changed to their boxers and vests and sat at various corners of the room giving importance to my presence in Delhi.

Thapa had changed a lot since the days he left school. He was more of Gen X type guy now against his boorish character at Dhanbad. I remembered how he used to go for morning shows every Sunday at Shri Krishna Talkies. His taste had changed from Lata Mangeshkar to Jennifer Lopez and from Hema Malini to Panelope Cruz. His music collections now mostly consists of pop, rock and Hard Metal bands rather than the soft melody of R D Burman of the past times. He now drank more beer than he used to drink Cola in the past.

Manu on the other hand had a good homeostasis. He adapted well without changing much. He was more focused and positive in his approach. May be his brother's presence had an impact.

But whatever the changes occurred, my buddies were still my buddies. They could understand my pain very well, may be a little less competent as far its origin was concerned. Looking at me cheerless for about half an hour Manu initiated, '*Chalo*, we will go around the University for a Stroll.'

'First we will take you to Miranda House. Nice girls there.' Thapa supported. Thapa's words made me to think whether he had turned out to be a sex maniac.

I faked a smile but was unable to disguise my feelings in front of my childhood buddies.

Manu came closer to me after smelling his armpits. He probably thought that I would be able to withstand the fragrance generated and put his arms across my shoulder.

'You have just come to Delhi. Enjoy for a week and then everything will be done. We have already decided what, when, how and where to approach.' Manu completed as if he consoled waving fingers across my dense hair.

Thapa clapped twice and threw a duplicate but nice Adidas T-shirt from his wardrobe to me. 'Fast, fast', He instructed like a sports trainer.

I smiled and followed his instructions. We left the Hostel and did a survey of the Kirori Mal College first. The red colored big building with patterns of brick was sufficient to provoke students to study there, leaving aside the rapport of the college. Big trees with benches were built to cater the needs of the paired electrons as we could see students still sitting on them. Every couple there reminded me of Ruchi.

As we came out of the college campus to the main road, I could figure out FMS, just opposite to KMC. 'This is among the 10 best business schools in India.' Manu described like a tour guide.

We gradually moved from Ramjas College to Hindu and St. Stephens as both constantly educated me with the standards of these colleges. My abilities looked dwarf in front of the students studying in them.

The promenade ended up at Kamala Nagar market for our dinner. They had discovered a fair price Parantha wala for their dinner away from the monotony of hostel mess. A cone of Vanilla Ice Cream from Mc Donalds priced Rs 7/- was chosen as a dessert.

All during the walkway I was comparing things and people. Though the girls were sexy, yet my emotions had overpowered my testosterone. I was actually missing Ruchi each time I was seeing a couple.

Reaching hostel, we went straight to Avikal Bhaiya's room. The motto was to figure out ways to get me enrolled.

'I think you decide about your choice of subject first.' Manu suggested.

'How about Political Science?' I said it just because Manu had the same subject and could help me out if required.

'Fine, the plan is to get you admitted in a south campus college initially and later migrate you to KMC.' Avikal Bhaiya said as if it was as easy as clapping.

'Get ready at 10.00 am tomorrow. We will meet the V.C.' He concluded and left.

Night soon switched over to morning and it progressed with homework for meeting with the Vice Chancellor. The designation itself was sufficient for me to melt my spine, forget the person.

I followed Avikal Bhaiya, dressed in formal attire, which I

later recognized was not required. The VC did not even bother to meet me.

'It's done. You will get admission to Ram Lal Anand college.' Avikal Bhaiya said boastingly as he came out of the VC's chamber. 'Things in India become so easy if you have a jack to raise you.' I thought.

Little relaxed from the ongoing stress, I returned to the hostel, but left again to Call Ruchi. I had to share the developments with her.

Actually I had called Jaya an hour back from a PCO near the VC'S office to convey Ruchi about my call. I wanted her only to pick my call up and no one else.

'Hello' Ruchi said in the same sweet voice.

'Kaisi ho?' I said, quite confident that it was Ruchi only.

'Fine. But I am missing you a lot. How about you, how are you?'

'Same here.'

'Did you have yourself enrolled?'

'Sort of. I mean it will be done tomorrow.'

'Good' She giggled. 'How are the girls in Delhi? I hope your retina is not fixed in any of them' I could smell jealousy in her tone as she said so.

'Nice yaar, I just can't get over those curves…..'

'Chup raho' she cut me short. 'I told you na, these Delhi bitches woo boys very easily'. A short-pitched slang followed.

'Are Baba, I was just kidding. How can I even think of someone else but you? Can I? Actually I love to see you jealous. You know, in all these days that I am away from you I have realized that how much I need you in my life. I can't stop thinking of you.'

'We will be together. Just have faith in God.' She supported.

'Okay, I will have to drop the phone. I am not carrying more money. Love You. Bye.'

'Love you too.' She said as our conversation ended like a well drafted speech of two politicians in conversation.

Charged up by Ruchi's words, I came back to the hostel and straightway browsed through the different textbooks scattered on Manu's study table. I started with a book on Political Science but my antennae could not catch its wavelength. It seemed like an overhead transmission.

I could nowhere relate them to the text of my past education. 'Let's start something new', I said to myself as I ended up with a book on Palmistry by Cheiro. Although it was tough to comprehend, yet it seemed like a better substitute than the Political Science book. Even Manu would have bought it for the same reason, I guessed.

Manu reached, so did Thapa, whistling and humming. His whistling tune and bright eyes were sufficient for me to judge that they knew about the proceedings with the VC.

'You're feeling better now?' Thapa asked.

'Nah, he can't be. See he is still doing research on those petite lines across the line of heart in his palm. Check if you can find something like 'R' etched. Manu said with overpowering sarcasm as he found me associated with the book of Palmistry. Both laughed in unison as they never wanted to lose a chance when it comes to pulling my leg with Ruchi as a reason.

The post-dinner session had its venue at Rahul's room. I liked the room firstly because it was erotically decorated and second, Bhaiya never visited there.

'I bet, I will get that *fachchi* to bed in seven days.' Rahul claimed as we entered.

Though I had learnt by then that *fachchi* meant First-year girl, yet the rest part of the sentence was alien to me. For others, it was the continuation of the dialogue they could not finish in the canteen.

Constant dedication to their conference came with an outcome that Rahul was pretty determined to use a girl for love-making, who initially denied even friendship owing respect to her present commitments.

Feeling useless and dejected there, unable to put my views on the topic, I came back to room. I also felt pity for Rahul as I was quite positive about the confidence the girl had in her commitments and that too without even knowing the girl at all.

* * *

Usual sunrise and sunsets completed days to follow. My solitude increased manifold as others were comparatively busier with their books than before. Cheiro's palmistry and Ruchi's photograph were now the integral part of my lifestyle, reading-through my palm with each page I go through.

The usual practice was disturbed with Bhaiya handing over an envelope enclosing a letter in it to me.

'Ram Lal Anand College, South Campus.' He paused. 'Tomorrow morning.....Go and meet the Principal. All your formalities will be completed tomorrow itself, carry all documents.' He ordered like a brigadier.

Like a tadpole in an ocean I somehow managed to swim to the specified address after cruising in the so called DTC buses. These buses were more overcrowded than in Dhanbad. 'People only blame Biharis', I thought.

There was one thing fairly good in these buses that the ticket fare gives you an additional 'Spa Treatment Package' free; most importantly, you have to avail it whether you want it or not. Sometime a heavy hand will massage your butt; otherwise you can see elbows playing billiards with bosoms.

The bus dropped me in the entrance of South Campus near Venkateshwara College. South campus...South Indian name, I tried to relate somewhere. As I progressed ahead I found many more colleges, though big, yet not as elegant as North Campus Colleges. The crowd, I must admit was still posh. The skirts of the babes around were shorter in length, and tops tight enough to reveal what they were supposed to hide. 'Maybe it had some equating relation with the cut off marks for admissions to these colleges.' I speculated.

The VC's letter in my hand erased all hesitations to enter the Ram Lal Anand College. Walking straight to the Administration department, I wondered whom to speak. It looked more like a Municipal Corporation Office where everybody was gloomy. I could not make out the authorities, until I found a peon. Thank God that somebody in the past had invented something called uniform. Yes, I saw him wearing a khaki color shirt and trouser, rubbing tobacco with his thumb on his palm. His style of doing it confirmed that he was a Bihari.

'Chacha,' I uttered using my past experience into practice.

'Haan beta', and I knew my job was done. I was helped by him to reach the Principal. Hearing my purpose of visit and looking at the envelope he took me to the Principal.

'Good morning Sir.' I said as I handed over the letter to the Principal. The VC's name on the envelope prompted him to read that instantly. I could see his marble like eyes scanning the letter as fast as a metal detector. Soon I was showered tremendous hospitality, more than what he would offer to his son-in-law.

Few calling bells and calls increased the speed of working in the administration department, as I found a fat-bellied man coming with different forms into the Principal's chamber.

'Complete his enrollment procedure now, and take care he is in Management quota.' The Principal ordered. I could read that the person was cursing me with stitched lips.

I returned back to hostel by similar means but wondered whether I should have asked for a drop back. Evaluating the situation in the Principal's chamber, it was not at all a lofty demand. I smiled, but on whom I didn't know.

I was happy to be a student of Delhi University now. Having an identity card of the college, I also got passes for daily travelling to south campus. Books were arranged by Manu, even all his notes were mine. With all those notes drafted by a University

Topper, I was least bothered to attend classes, far there at Ram Lal Anand.

A periodic conversation with Ruchi was always on the cards. I also conveyed to my parents of the support offered by Avikal Bhaiya to me. 'He did a lot for me.' I thought. I was perhaps wrong in thinking that. The major part was yet to come.

Amidst crackers and fireworks around, Avikal Bhaiya towed me like a sheep by a shepherd, on the Diwali eve. The fantastic light decorations and the fireworks were not competent enough to grab my attention as I wondered where I was heading to, until I noticed a nice bungalow decorated with *diyas*.

'This is our Principal Sir's home.' He said as I knew where I was but was again in a dilemma whether he was my Principal as well.

'Can't he make things simpler for me; he should have told me all this earlier; he is trying to prove how over smart he is.' And many immediate notions cropped up in my mind for *Bhaiya*, forgetting all his help. Stupid selfish mind of mine, *Bhaiya* was least aware of them.

Disgusted with the thoughts within, I could see him touching the feet of a dark complexioned, bald man. He had some white hair on his ear lobes to nullify the greed of his scalp. Maybe he did not trim them for some self-assurance.

When my eyes went down further down the toes, I too followed suit with Bhaiya. It was my need that provoked me to do so rather than some feelings of respect.

'Come inside.' He said with a smile.

We entered and plunged ourselves in a sofa and were soon presented with colorful sweets. The sweets encouraged me to pick them all but I sustained.

'Sir. He is my brother's friend I told you about.' Bhaiya said to the Principal munching a piece of Laddoo. The statement revealed that everything was discussed earlier and I was there just for the icing on the cake.

'What is your name?' he asked.

'Aniruddha.......Aniruddha Trivedi.' I said stressing on the full name later.

He smiled hearing my name. *Bhaiya* reciprocated with a smile. I looked ignorant. I never found my name funny but I never knew that my Surname had the power to drift me to places, of course to both extremes. I wondered whether that was the only important reason to know the name of any candidate in an interview.

'Possibly Aniruddha will attend classes at KMC from next Monday.' Bhaiya announced in front of Thapa and Manu as we returned to hostel. Everybody rejoiced. Yet another celebration was waiting for us in the night. Diwali delight was increased with my placement. Each one had their selection of brands and mixes and was high by the time the party reached to climax. I too was high but Ruchi's thought were probably the culprit and not those pegs of Blender's Pride.

'Let's go to Vaishno Devi' Thapa suggested and in no delay everybody endorsed. Perhaps the guilt of having alcohol had propelled it.

❉ ❉ ❉

The next couple of days passed steadily with no great fuss, until I was with Manu at the Mc Donalds for ice creams.

'Meet her. She is Neha, First year, Political Science, from Jamshedpur.' He introduced me to a girl already present there. My nervousness in these situations were evidently proved when I swallowed the swirl of ice cream rather than licking it

'And he is Aniruddha, tomorrow onwards he will join in KMC'. 'Political Science' he said the later part slowly and smiled. 'You will be a company to Aniruddha in the class.' He ordered as I felt embarrassed.

She smiled. Maybe it was for the order but I thought it was for my inability to eat ice cream.

I could not accompany Manu and others for the visit to the holy shrine the next evening.

'Get some Prasad and Vaishnao Devi pendants for me' I told to them as they were about to board an auto near the hostel gate.

'Pendant for whom?' Thapa asked with some irony.

'Don't ask stupid questions. Does he need to specify the name Ruchi.' Stronger blows of pun kept coming from Manu.

It was a cakewalk for me to get inside KMC. Few confident strides down the hostel, along the walls with recently concluded student's union elections posters escorted me to the classroom. Neha was spotted right at the door, maybe she was waiting for me only. People looked at me as if some alien had landed straight from outer space, barring some hostelites, with whom I was little familiar, though up to the extent of a smile and 'Hi' only. My confident legs were no more confident.

Neha draped in a white salwar Kameez, provided me the maximum hospitality that she could afford. Modest know-how with some classmates happened under Neha's jurisdiction, yet I was little embarrassed to cite reason for my late entry. I wished I could skip this part as I felt it tougher than the ragging.

Though I exploited my full concentration in the political atmosphere of the class and also into the notes at room, yet I had a rather tough time with the Political theory. Neha assisted me where ever she could but I otherwise considered the complex formula of Deoxy Ribonucleic Acid and twisted diagram of digestive system of cockroach easier than that.

Nothing apart from Neha's friendship boosted me in the classroom. I had shared everything with Neha, even about Ruchi.

'Even I have my love at Jamshedpur and I love him a lot.' Neha's shy voice entered my ears.

Manu and others were back. I was still dwelling as an unauthorized immigrant in the KMC hostel, room no 29. With 15 days into the college, I still could not justify my selection of subject. I shared all these woes with Neha but not with Ruchi as in the later case it might change perceptions, but in former it did not matter.

It was a cloudy Wednesday morning. Everything seemed same in the college except the fact that Neha was not present. She had been to a far relative's place in Badarpur for some occasion as she had detailed me with, a day before. Monotony surfaced on my face. 'A chat with Ruchi can give some respite.' I thought and left the classroom right after the first period.

'All lines to this route are busy, please call after some time' continuously chanted from the phone each time I dialed her number until I decided to hang up. I searched for other options to kill time and decided to go to Rahul. He was a champion in bunking classes.

Happy to see it bolted from inside, I approached to knock but averted myself hearing a feminine voice. With an increase in heart beat, I was expecting a live show as I peeped inside through the cracks near the hinges. 'What else could be the best remedy for boredom?' I thought.

My entire thrill collapsed when I found through the fringe crack that the girl was Neha. Rahul was not only kissing her as I could see both of them getting under the blanket all nude. They were making love.

I came to my room with aches in my heart and soul. 'She must have been the facchi, they were discussing that day, but why the hell did Neha get into all these? She is committed after all. If all men are Bastards, what are women?' I asked myself.

The scrutiny of Neha's morale gave me a sedative dose. The ample mass inside my skull was divided into two groups now. The first set of infinite neurons whispered each other 'Ruchi is also like that.'

'Can't be; Neha is a slut and not everyone is like that,' retaliated others. I shut my eyelids to keep these conversations within the perimeter of my pain. They continued to shoot, however.

For me words like love, faith, promises etc. had emptied themselves off their meanings yet unquestionably they sounded right whenever Ruchi's face surfaced into my thoughts. I felt like a chicken which had been skinned and marinated without being slaughtered.

'What's up? Looking much tensed!' Manu questioned as he entered in the evening.

I was not in a condition to explain things to myself, forget Manu.

'How was the class today? I asked I probably thought that a question as silly as that would be the perfect answer. I was of course able to disguise Manu who was infested with the boring lectures at the college.

The deserted terrace up through the dim lit stairs offered the ideal ambience for the wrestle within my cranium to flourish further. My nerve cells were equally divided over the issue. I needed few more so that I could I reach to a final conclusion. I decided to divert my mind 'Can those extra nerve cells not be of Manu's? No, if there is any it can be only of Ruchi's' I answered to myself.

Energized by the decision I hopped down the stairs to the room. The 'Indian Railways Time Table' in my hands in place of the Cheiro's book shocked everybody. I feel that my decision go back Dhanbad was firm enough as nothing could divert me. My career woes; Bhaiya's influence and initiative to get me admitted; Manu's friendship… all weighed less if compared with Ruchi.

'I am sorry Yaar.' I said to Manu.

He smiled and patted. 'Gaandu' He said.. Though I don't understand your woes here, yet I won't stop you. And listen say my 'Hi' to Ruchi. He smiled again with those intentionally created wrinkles across his face to hide sadness.

Thapa hugged me with the 'MANCHESTER UNITED' jersey on him, but the heart throbbing inside was still *'desi'* and emotionally rich. *Bhaiya* did not come out to see me off.

I left the campus in an auto to the railway station, New Delhi this time. There were no homemade sweetmeats, reserved berth but an eagerness to meet Ruchi.

I clinched a deal with one of the porter whose associates would block unreserved seats right there at the yard itself.

'Fifty Rupees for the singlet window chair.' He said finally as if announcing a death sentence. I tried fooling him after occupying the seat, but just the mere thought of his curses and there effects on my relationship with Ruchi prompted me to take out a fifty rupee note of my wallet, from where the hidden passport size photograph of Ruchi seemed as if it smiled at my idiotic moves.

The compartment was completely packed like trucks carrying herds of goats. One good thing it did was that it increased the temperature inside against the otherwise chilly weather outside. I was almost lost in woes, worries, happiness, tensions which would come to me at periodic intervals, quite in sync with the farts around. I could smell Radish sometimes but mostly it was tough to guess the raw material used in making the delicacy.

The pantry car servers never visited the general compartment. I wished there was some Gujrati or South Indian family who could help me out in the dinner from their gigantic tiffin boxes they usually carried. But against my wish the train carried mostly Bengalis, who never carried food. They search for reasons to eat out, so what if it was a railway platform.

A SPOILT SOUP

*J*finally reached Dhanbad the next day at noon. An obvious exclamation welcomed me at home. It was really tough for me to logically disowm a theory which I gave to go to Delhi. Silence prevailed among all my uncles depicting unhappiness as I sipped tea in the afternoon.

'I want to give medicals yet another try.' I said. Everybody approved with expecting expressions.

I had not yet met Ruchi. A small call to Jaya arranged for a meet.

Jaya dropped Ruchi at the Bank More, leaving her alone to mingle with me in private. My pupil remained dilated and lips stretched as I could spot Ruchi from the opposite side of the road. The traffic was ransacked for a minute as I tried to cross the road amidst heavy and gruesome horns. Ruchi's expressions changed like traffic signals and ended up in a pretty smile, the smile which forced me to come back from Delhi.

`I pulled her towards the restaurant called 'THE HOST'. Ordering for Coffee in the otherwise vacant restaurant, I constantly focused on her eyes. Taking the Vaishnao Devi Pendant out of my pocket, I hooked it around her neck. The waiter gazed continuously, confused.

I narrated the entire Delhi episode and my reasons to come back. She could not actually express her feelings verbally but soon I found her eye liner dripping down the cheeks.

'You don't have that faith in me?' She shook her head sideways as tears sprinkled on her lap. I recognized my guilt. I felt like to take out all those neurons inside the skull which prompted me to think so, and burn them. I could not do that.

I did what the same neurons directed me at that time. I hugged Ruchi and tears came out of my eyes as well.

'I love you shona, I can't live without you.' I whispered in her ears. 'I can't dream of a life without you and this is the outcome of that only. Please forgive me.' I added.

'*Chalo coffee piyo*' She said. We detached and inched towards the cups.

She agreed to my decision of going for medicals again but only if with full dedication.

'We will not meet until exams.' She announced. It was tough for me to do so being in Dhanbad, but I too somewhere gazed the seriousness of the situation.

Physics, chemistry and Biology once again were the priority. Jaya was the transmitter for any communication between us, which was almost seized, not because of any other reason but to change focus to studies.

The entrance examination that year, the results to follow, and time had different plans. Neither of us could get through. It was long that we spoke to each other.

The biggest ever stun of my life came in form of Sid's words.

Amidst the crowd in the PCO, Sid's voice echoed in my ears- 'Forget her. She is not the one who loves you. Better you focus on your career now.'

'Pagal hai kya? Stop Joking' I replied in a trouble-free tone.

'I wish I could have.' 'Ruchi has told Jaya about her decision.' He added after a pause.

'But why? What decision?' I felt baffled. 'It can be yet another hiccup in this love story. I will sort it out.' I thought. Things like this were not happening for the first time.

With all these uncertainties only Ruchi's words could have been savior. Call to her home sometimes ended with Kroorsingh's roar; otherwise there was a recurring of 'HELLO's.

That made me feel tensed. 'Was Sid right? Does she want it to be over? How can she?'

It was tough to measure my distress. Something unbelievable had hit my ear drum. The infinite set of neurons started spying- sometimes Sid's intensions; sometimes Jaya's. Leena, Samit…. and everybody linked with both of us were scanned by them, but the needle never pointed to Ruchi.

Sleep was lost. I was just lying on bed.

Jaya still continued to be my friend. Ruchi started pursuing some degree in IT and I was informed by Jaya.

A meet with Ruchi could have disclosed facts, but she evaded me at her institute. She departed in front of me as if she had never known me. I was somewhere wrong in spying others.

Devoid of an estimated career and a morale support I headed for the Hotel Management at Bhubaneswar.

WITH GROUP OF CHEFS
REPAIR WORK in BHUBANESWAR

'*N*ice and good story' Kaustav said. 'Isn't it a little in-complete?'

It took three rounds of tea at Cafeteria, evening snacks and the dinner to complete the story. It was 3.00 am in the morning when Aniruddha ended.

'So, you guys broke up? Kaustav added.

'Dunno… but surely there is a crack… visible enough.' Aniruddha claimed.

'But why didn't you call her after then. She could be waiting for you.' I questioned.

'I told you that I did all sorts of things. I feel she is not interested.'

'So you have concluded and this is why the post break-up depression?'

'Listen Aniruddha, you need to be practical. Either you work on this situation or get out of it.' I added.

'I guess you should move on. She has stopped thinking of you. She is fine with herself. She is in a new college, may have new friends and who knows what she is doing there… and what you are doing is ruining yourself. If you have forgotten, let me remind you of your capabilities. That fucking Sahu is boasting around that he would be the topper this year. Don't you understand where he stands in front of you?' Kaustav tried to uplift Aniruddha.

'And yes, that chic – Shilpa, looks interested in you. She keeps asking me about your whereabouts every time I inch towards her. Gosh... she has damn sexy thighs. I wish I were you.' Kaustav tried to pinch in some humor.

For the next few days we meticulously tried every technique to move ahead, but we failed. Teas, breakfast, lunch, dinner all had the same topic of discussion.

'You know Aniruddha, you have become a boring company. If you continue doing so, she will change her idea of coming back even she decides for it.' Kaustav initiated. 'Anyways, what is the last update?'

'Yes, what's the status now? I mean the latest fact. I uttered as if explaining Kaustav's words.

Aniruddha closed his eyes and uttered nothing. His eyelids tightened and his right fist punched his left palm. He took his spects out.

'What? Is she married?' Kaustav guessed. 'Get over her man.'

'No.' He just gestured. 'She is not yet married and she is in Bhubaneswar for her B.Sc IT. Jaya called for to keep me informed about the same.' Aniruddha spoke in an otherwise low volume.

'What? She is in Bhubaneswar, she is not yet married, you know it all......and you are....... Shit! You know what; you are an Ass, rather Dumb Ass.' Kaustav looked puzzled.

'She loves you man. Why the hell is she coming to Bhubaneswar for her B.Sc IT. People look for Hyderabad and Bangalore and not Bhubaneswar. You just approach her. Understand the whole funda.' Kaustav was swift in concluding facts.

'Anyways, where is she putting up? I mean which college?'

'I don't know.'

'Then find out. This cold blooded attitude is freaking me out.'

'I wish I could. I have no clues nor does Jaya.' Aniruddha surrendered.

Two hours later we were walking towards the Internet Café. Kaustav was pretty much a regular visitor there. Thanks to the rediffmail account he had recently signed up and also to the few porn sites known to him.

All of us got inside a cabin meant for one or maximum up to two persons at an extra rate. Kaustav was fiddling with the keys in the key board and we were expecting a nude blonde with ample bosoms.

A few seconds of silence hung over us, and we finally looked at the 14 inch screen with our jaws open. List of Information Technology colleges in Bhubaneswar popped up. We were ecstatic. Aniruddha kissed Kaustav. Tears seemed to overflow Aniruddha's eyes.

'I am not always a bad guy.' Kaustav mocked.

'You are never' and both hugged each other.

That day my whole perception towards Kaustav changed. He was the usual guy, a little more freaking and careless. But when it came to support, he was a better man.

'Where were you?' Kaustav asked Aniruddha. We were talking for the first time in the day, right in the evening.

'I was trying to find her out. What else?'

'So how's it going? I told you, you will get her back. It might be little difficult but your prize is premium as well.' Kaustav said.

Kaustav and I looked at Aniruddha, till he smiled.

'Yes, I browsed four colleges of the city and got a slight hint in the last one. If all goes well. I guess I will trace her out'

'But how?' Kaustav was excited.

'It was not that tough as I had guessed. These private institutes are greedy to take in more and more students.'

'So?'

'I went to the institutes and asked them whether I can get my sister migrated, who is currently studying at Dhanbad to their college. All the institutes said yes, baring the last one who also added that a similar migration took place recently from Dhanbad. Also they have a girls Hostel.' Aniruddha explained.

'Then...' was prompted further in unison.

'It seemed that she was in that institute. I pretended not to be convinced and asked if could speak to that candidate. Their answer was negative but they have assured me that they would give me her number with her consent. Now I am just hoping for the same.' Aniruddha added.

'Does that mean you would start talking to Ruchi again?' I asked

'I don't know whether I would be able to do so or not, but I will surely try to understand why she broke up with me.' Aniruddha replied.

'All is good if you make yourself capable enough for her also. Remember, you need to be at least a Sous Chef in three years, and that's not very easy. Also Professor Acharya has asked about you three times in the last week.' I reminded him of the classes as well.

Things were not that easy as Aniruddha was pretending it to be. Visible changes were noticed in his character and he was willing for some in his appearance too.

A sly guy from the college prescribed him couple of pills which would assist him in gaining weight. He was only 60 Kgs in his 6 feet frame. So fanatically, he decided to look better and impress Ruchi and so he took them from him without the wrapper at insanely high prices. The guy actually did not want him to know the name of the medicine.

And yes, it showed results. Within the weekend his cheeks were puffed like a Burger bun and the skeleton started to accumulate some adipose beneath the skin. If not a Bolywood Hero, he was not a sidekick of the villain anymore.

But everything comes with a price. His dinner now comprised of at least 16 chapatis, 2 Dal Tadka, 2 Egg Bhurji. Still he used to search for biscuits in the midnight. Breakfast and lunch were still to follow.

It would have been good if that was the only concern though. He woke up at 11.00 am.

'Oh Fuck! How can it be? The alarm..... Did it ring? Where is everybody? And Kaustav?' Plenty of questions with no answers sped on his mind. The fragrance coming out from his underarms prompted him to take shower. By the time he reached the college it was already lunch time. The food for him was very precious and he directly headed towards the dining hall. With the ring of the next bell he was right there- the first in the queue to take lunch.

The quantity of Payasam in his plate provoked him to squeeze his eyebrows. The eyes looked even smaller with his puffed up cheeks.but he could not say a word. The professor was standing next to the server and desserts were as always limited.

He sat down quickly to gulp the first serve and joined the queue again for the second. With heaps of Jeera rice, dal and Paneer lababdar he settled only to be spotted by everybody eating like flood victims.

Kaustav tracing Aniruddha, picked a chair near him, and gave him a stern look at his idiocy.

'Seems like u have not eaten for years, dude! Try to behave yourself'. Kaustav was sad hearing what the others were commenting.

'What behavior are you talking about? And where were you? Why did not you wake me up?'

'I was in college only and for your kind information I tried waking you up, not once but several times but you slept as if you have taken marijuana.'

Aniruddha found it better not to argue. He completed with a 'Don't know how this is happening' face.

Soon they were in their classroom for their next subject, Hotel Engineering.

The classroom seemed blurred for Aniruddha as they sat next to each other. Though Kaustav was holding his hand, jerking him frequently, he failed to keep him awake right there in the first row.

Everyone stood up when the professor entered but Aniruddha. Nobody dared to blink, focused, sitting straight with their spines perpendicular to the seat. Aniruddha was in his own world. Mr.Siddheshwar Swain, an M.Tech from IIT Kharagpur was there to teach Engineering to students who would basically deal with switching ON/OFF their MCBs to the maximum.

An extended lecture on the definition of Ampere and the class was over. He spontaneously stopped his lecture with the bell and reached to Aniruddha to shake his head. Thankfully he woke up against expectations.

'Aniruddha, I took the class on defining one ampere. You were sleeping, but I have given you the attendance' he told very calmly of which Aniruddha perceived nothing.

'He is not well sir.' Kaustav stood for Aniruddha.

The professor shook his head and left.

Kaustav had done all possible exercises, positively or negatively then to change Aniruddha but all in vain. No movies, no bunking classes, no late night gossips and the typical countrymen attire. But all required was a hint of Ruchi back in his life and he was the most impressive guy around. Girls, most of whom used to call him Aniruddha *Bhaiya*, repented now.

Though Kaustav managed to trace out the name of the pills Aniruddha was taking, by rallying around a chemist, and stopped him to take those, still the glow was not lost. Not that the pills had left the mark, it was the allusion of getting Ruchi back which was doing wonders.

*

Everything looked uneventful around in the pretext of Aniruddha. All he was waiting for was a call from that IT College with Ruchi's contact number. He waited for an opportunity to speak with Ruchi. 'It was just that his pretty love was in little confusion or dilemma or little anger, but he would wipe them all in the first meet.' He thought.

And he received a call. Kaustav phone was doing wonders and was always at Aniruddha's possession.

'Can I speak to Aniruddha?' A male voice asked.

'Speaking.' He said promptly thinking it to be some official from the college.

'You have so damn transformed. So busy that you can't call me, ever once. Huh. Where do you stay? Tell me. I am coming right now.' He said it all in a stretch as if it was practiced dialogue.

It did nothing more than to put Aniruddha shocked. Who is this? Official????? How does he know me and showing so much proximity.......or Ruchi????? What happened to her voice........ was this the reason she stopped talking?

'Didn't you recognize me or what?

'No...I mean Yes. You are....' Aniruddha could not complete.

'Siddhartha. I guess the name will be enough.'

Aniruddha was in an intricate situation, swinging in between exclamatory and interrogatory body languages

'No. actually I was expecting a call and my psyche was very much into that. Anyways how are you and where you are? I agree that I did not call you all these days but so did you. And with me, you I guess know the reason.' Aniruddha defended in an attacking mode.

'Forget it all; just message me your address in this number. Now'. He commanded with urgency.

Couple of hours and there was a knock at our door. Aniruddha jumped to open the door and a cute chocolaty hero type guy stepped in. Greetings started with slangs between them.

Siddhartha looked quite similar as Aniruddha discussed earlier.

'Nice place.' He said as if he had to say something...anything, or maybe it was pun intended. He glanced around the room in which three of us were dwelling. Three soft mattresses, lying parallel to each other at one corner of the room with mosaic flooring. Few hefty books stacked on each other, placed near the pillow. LARROUSSE GASTRONOMIQUE read the one on top. Between the pages a 4*6 photo was used as a bookmark. 'So, what had you been doing all these years?'

'Hotel Management.....Trying to be a chef.'

'I can see that.' His eyes moved towards the books. 'You can call Jaya, but not me.' He complained.

Siddhartha had been doing engineering all these days, and had just joined Satyam Computers at Bhubaneswar.

'Hope you have got over her.' Sid said to him, pointing at the book and then looking at us. He was confident whose photograph it can be. He saw Aniruddha doing that earlier, regularly.

We smiled and Sid had his answer.

'Listen Aniruddha. You should move on. She has stopped calling, neither she receive calls. She does not feel it important to share why is she doing this all. She is fine with herself I guess. May be there is something, someone…I don't know. Don't know where is she? Doing What?'

'I know where she is.' And he detailed. There was excitement in his eyes in doing so.

'That's just being so optimistic. The institute can never provide you with anybody's contact details, that too of a girl staying in the hostel.' Sid was against the idea. 'You better move on. I have heard the chicks in Hotel Management colleges are too hot' he smiled.

Kaustav chipped in. Now he found Sid interesting. 'So where are you putting up at?'

'Jaydev Vihar'

'Nice. Nice place' Kaustav returned the favor.

Aniruddha started feeling weak with his ideas. General discussion on love, lust and life followed and all the way Ruchi was in use as an instance. He leaned back. He had to control his urge to shout. Upset with the subject, Aniruddha resigned from the debate and headed for some tea. Everyone trailed, as for them the connecting link was missing.

It was not long that he waited for a call from Ruchi's institute. Recollecting his emotions and boosting his moral he was back in business. It was Friday, I remember- a strategically chosen one by Aniruddha. Armed with his silly plan to woo the principal, he went to the IT College. SATYA SAI INSTITUTE OF TECHNOLOGY.

'Can you please give me the contact number of the girl recently migrated from Dhanbad?' Aniruddha was bang on target.

'How silly is that! I mean that's not possible.' The principal- a lady, tried to maintain her calm.

'But I was promised this by one of your clerks'. Didn't he?

'May be he had. But we can't do it now.' She said straight forward. 'Moreover, you have not yet shown the papers of the candidate you want to get migrated and from which college?' she presented a 'How is that possible' look. 'Thank you.' She ended.

'Unpleasant creature.' Aniruddha thought.

The principal's last sentence was long enough for Aniruddha to feel insulted and short enough to get inside of him and melt his positives out.

As he turned back and took strides towards the door, she saw a group of girls pass by. He sensed it. It was Ruchi. The girl who migrated from Dhanbad was Ruchi. Even the mitochondria of his cells were familiar with her. He was elated, but the time was not on his side. Should he speak, should he not? The situation was hanging around, mocking him and daring him and then slowly creeping inside before you can get your act together.

As he came out everybody vanished.

He hurried back to IHM, only to get even more depressed. He was not allowed to enter the college. Actually no one, for that new rule imposed by our principal to be in campus before 9.15 am.

Aniruddha was restless. He wanted to get this stress out of his system. Somebody who would lend his ear to vomit whatever he had witnessed at the IT College. He didn't have Kaustav's cell phone either.

He hopped into an auto and guided the driver. The auto driver zipped through the highway, took few lefts and rights, and finally reached into a very big building, looked as if made of glass. SATYAM it was.

'Siddhartha Banerjee' He enquired with the security.

Few rounds of security checks followed and he was allowed to reach in the reception. Soon Sid arrived.

'What happened? All of a sudden!' Sid was surprised.

Aniruddha was gasping. He took water and then narrated, unable to understand whether to feel happy or sad.

'I have said it before and am saying now, GET OVER HER. I have got few indications from Jaya which compels me to say this. She, for you, is just a mirage.' Sid by being strict, tried to bring Aniruddha to normalcy.

A minute of silence and Aniruddha replied. 'I will get over her. Just make me speak to her once. I just wanted to clarify, from her, in her words. What made her to do so?'

'Okay I will, but you have to promise you will never try to get in touch with her after this.' Sid sounded convincing.

Aniruddha nodded.

'Come to my flat sometime in the evening.' Sid cheered Aniruddha with his thumbs up.

Aniruddha, willing to push the sun down the horizon, to let the evening set in, to rush to Sid, to get the issues cleared. He was still optimistic of the outcome.

Unable to face the anxiety, he called up Jaya.

'Hey… what happened? You met Sid… enjoying?' Jaya asked.

'Hmmm… under the circumstances, yes.' He said

'What circumstances?'

'I met Ruchi.....I mean saw her. Felt like meeting her, speak to her.' Aniruddha was desperate.

'You will never change. But she is coming back to Dhanbad, probably today, at least for a week I suppose.

'Oh I see. This is all because... I think you understand. At least you.' Aniruddha confined within himself the fact of calling her. Perhaps he did not want anyone to stop him from that.

Aniruddha closed his eyes and started summing up the events with Ruchi. Everything that was good and everything not so good too. For him the latter didn't exist. He was very keen to call her, but a call today might not give proper effect. He will wait, he decided, at least for a couple of days, till she settles back at her house in these vacations.

And on the very third day he bounced back to Sid. 'Hey' He swung the already opened door along the hinges.

Sid smiled; already busy talking to somebody over phone in Bengali. Perhaps Jaya. He was talking about reaction, behavior and love; quite possible all about Aniruddha and Ruchi. For them it was important. It all started together.

'Ruchi is in Dhanbad now and Jaya has agreed to share her cell number only for this call.' Aniruddha nodded. He was being impatient. He would have agreed for anything at this point.

Siddhartha took his cell phone and again dialed a number. 'Calling Ruchi' the screen displayed.

'Hello' and Aniruddha started feeling cold under his feet and palms. His face sweating and heart racing.

'Hi Ruchi. Sid here. How are you? Just got your number from Jaya. Heard you are studying in Bhubaneswar! Even I am posted here at Satyam.' Aniruddha was willing him to be straight, talking about him and not what he was doing.

'Great!!!' She replied.

'Anyways, there is something else as well. Aniruddha is with me and wants to speak to you.' He replied.

'Hmmm... I know. I saw him in my college that day.' 'There

is something I need to tell him.' She completed. Sid handed over the phone to Aniruddha. She must have discussed about that with Jaya earlier.

Aniruddha looked at the phone as if Ruchi's face was visible in it and later placed it near his ear lobes. 'Kaisi ho?' he asked with uncertainty.

'Good, and you?' She replied. Aniruddha took a deep breath in.

'Where have you been? Where? Leaving me alone like this. You know na, I can't live without you. Can I?' His eyes were getting moist with each word.

'There is something that I need to tell you, that I haven't told earlier, something I was eager to tell all these days.' She was bold enough.

Now she had something to tell. Aniruddha wished she had nothing to say like…. 'I love someone else' or 'My marriage is set.' He prayed to god within that time that it should be something at least repairable. 'Tell me. ' His voice crumbled.

'Papa could not believe that I could not make it to medicals. It was his dream that I had broken. You know he had expectations from me as a son and I….. could not live up to that. He started behaving bizarre and I started feeling guilty. Soon others including you were placed somewhere on the other but me. I took up IT as a career, but that also is under downfall. I really want to prove myself in front of my papa. I don't know in achieving this goal, I might keep you waiting….till I succeed…might not return even…..that would be unfair. Hence I camouflaged.' She completed.

Aniruddha was lost, unable to settle on whether he should be happy or sad. 'But whatever you did, even that was not fair. Isn't it?' he questioned. 'What you thought, it will be too easy for me to manage? Stupid.' He expressed his displeasure, whatever he could.

'I am sorry. It was just that ….I am sorry. Please don't ruin your life.'

'I will wait for you till you come back. Till you succeed. Can I?' Aniruddha made a half hearted effort to ignore the turmoil in his heart.

She could not reply, probably choked on her tears, as Aniruddha thought, or maybe she did not want to.

'Can I meet you once? Only once.' Aniruddha pleaded.

'Yes' she replied. 'I will be back next Friday. See you then.'

'At Ram Mandir, next Sunday, 10.00am' Aniruddha said and she confirmed.

'You are a nice guy Aniruddha. I am sorry.' She said.

'There is nothing worse than running from yourself. I know you love me and so do I. Ask yourself about this. I know you will be back. Take care. Bye.' And the phone was disconnected

*

'Where the hell is my Blue shirt?' Aniruddha shouted as he was digging into the same VIP suitcase which he was using since few years now.

Yes, the same blue shirt, which Ruchi has gifted her, the same one with which he wanted to disguise his uncle but failed. Though he never used to wear that, still it was always in his suitcase wherever it goes. May be he had kept it for occasion like this.

'Shit!'He remembered he had put it in Kaustav's suitcase when he took his for a repairing to the nearby *mistry*.

It was a Sunday and probably 7.00 a.m but night enough for Aniruddha to continue his nap. But today he woke up at 5.30 am and tried to get himself ready. It was more important than any meeting or interview. He was going to meet Ruchi as planned. He was sure he would get her back in her life after this meet.

Not being a part of the morning tea on a Sunday at Manoj's Restaurant, he rather preferred to take a bath. A long, shampooed one today. By 8.30 he was already dressed in convincing attire. The Navy Blue shirt tucked precisely inside his khaki trouser, and hold well with the Italian leather belt he had borrowed from Kaustav. Unlike usual, he did not forget to carry his handkerchief. 'It shows that you are responsible' he remembered his mother quoting that, time and again.

And yes, he was going to prove the same today to her. That he is eligible enough, willing enough to take her responsibilities.

Kaustav brought some tea from him. Aniruddha ran from one corner of the untidy room in a crazy excitement, trying to check all the things he had planned before leaving. Happy; anticipating the good to come, his eyes became moist.

'I firmly believe everything to be smooth soon.' Kaustav said pouring the still warm tea from a plastic sachet, he brought from Manoj. Handing over the plastic cup to Aniruddha he said, 'just hope she doesn't ditches you.' Somewhat contradicting what he said earlier, he completed.

Aniruddha took the tea, gave it a deep look and kept it back on the floor. Not that the tea was cold, or he was perturbed by Kaustav's second statement. It was just that he wanted to offer a prayer. Fasting was in his mind. He was still optimistic.

He left the room with ample time in his possession. He wanted to be on time or rather before time. Reaching the main road he grabbed an auto, and bowed before every temple, mosque or any hint of anything related to god throughout his twenty five minutes journey.

The temple was cleaned. He had visited this temple once earlier. It had a big lobby, just in front of the idol of Shri Rama, Laxmana and Sita. He bowed before god, and offered his prayer. He had nothing new to ask for. All that he was asking since last couple of years is same. Even god knew that.

After taking the *prasad,* he parked himself on the carpet at the lobby, concentrating into the eyes of lord Rama. They were satisfied. Aniruddha wanted the same.

Gradually people came, and they went. Aniruddha still waiting. It was 10.30 am and Ruchi still not arrived. Aniruddha could not digest the fact the she was not coming. 'May be she got up late or some hostel problems' He said to himself.

He moved fanatically across the lobby, diagonally, zigzag. He moved out to the shoe stand and back to temple but he could not find Ruchi. 'What should he do?' he asked himself. 'Did she forget the venue, the date.......or me?' he was tensed. He again walked straight to lord, looked into those charmed eyes.

'You look tensed. Come here.' A heavy voice echoed. It was a *sadhu*. He signaled Aniruddha inside. 'Whatever happens is at the will of god, and that is always right. If something has not happened today, it might happen tomorrow! You never know.'

All it did was that it gave little poise to Aniruddha's anxiety. He touched his feet and left. It was 2.00 pm when he reached his room.

Kaustav opened the door with an interrogation in his face. 'Met her? Talked? How's she?' He was hoping everything to be encouraging.

Aniruddha took a deep breath to slow down his heart beat. Though intangibly Ruchi was always with him, but he wanted her tangible presence in his life. 'She could not make it to this meet, probably some issues in the hostel.' Aniruddha defended Ruchi.

Kaustav shook his head in despair, and said nothing. Perhaps his act said everything he wanted to say.

Aniruddha didn't bother. He made it a point to visit the temple every Sunday at 10.00am. 'Talking with that Sadhu gives a relief' he was heard saying to Kaustav. But why 10.00 am and only on Sundays that too in the same attire, everybody knew.

He was a regular face in the temple now. With passing days he started to bring in his 'Theory of Cookery' book along so that while waiting he can read some 'cuts of beef, pork and lamb and chicken'. Nobody disturbed him there for doing so, apart from Ruchi's thoughts. But Ruchi...........she never turned up. Neither did Aniruddha call her again.

✳

It was late in the evening when he woke up yawning to see his batch mates gathering. Words like Training, internship, OJT, Specialization and their synonyms were echoing inside the cubical structure of bricks which we called room.

Everybody including Kaustav and I were excited about our forthcoming Industrial Exposure Training. Each one managed to sneak into some or the other hotel courtesy various sources. The training was supposed to be ruthless as described by seniors and was yet another situation like pre ragging periods. 'Excessive working hours', 'no fun' were some logics which were defended by 'exposure', 'learning' etc. The only thing common in the discussion was that everybody was favoring bigger and branded hotels against the smaller counterparts.

'Are you all discussing something as important as ....' Aniruddha asked in an open-ended manner.

'As important as what?' Somebody replied back.

'Love', replied the other. Everybody laughed in mockery as all of them knew of his tale and wanted him to come out of it.

Nothing helped. We only ended up like that but he was as callous as ever.

There was one more creature, who was not that ecstatic about the training. Ashish. Not that he was in love or something, but just not bothered. A small, silent personality with his hair constantly under erosion.

Not many things were common between them but their domicile. Yes, he was from Dhanbad too. Some 2 Kms away from Aniruddha's place. All they had dealt with earlier was using each other as courier and messengers to their home. Life for him was as bland as a boiled and mashed Potato, neither seasoned nor flavored. A sachet of gutkha in his back pocket, with incredible consistency in his brand. He along with Aniruddha were still to be placed for their industrial training.

'Can I have both of your resume'? Kaustav asked. I don't understand why these two *dheelas* are in our group.

Everybody condemned these two to inspire them for the training initiatives. 'Baba, if you will not do anything for it, then ....' And someone farted. Topic changed. Everybody blamed the other and the court was adjourned for the day, or rather he evening.

The next day came as a relief for the entire gang as everybody including Aniruddha and Ashish were placed in some hotel or another. The institute provided assistance in placements in training and Aniruddha and Ashish were placed in a small three star hotel in Bhubaneswar itself.

No matter it was just for 22 weeks that we were being separated, we started missing each other. Few of us were in same city or may be in same hotels, started nurturing plans. Train tickets were reserved and we left, leaving Aniruddha and Ashish in Bhubaneswar.

Their training started and for them it was more of personal development than exposure in the department allotted. If Aniruddha fooled the Housekeeping supervisor, praising of her beauty, Ashish deceived the stewards that he can teach them better about beverage service. And sometimes when Ashish was busy handling banquets, Aniruddha was busy cleaning rooms and commodes too.

Departments changed, time elapsed, and finally both were in the same department. Their chosen one, Food Production or Kitchen as you understand. They worked hard. Harder. Did everything from peeling gunny bags of onions to making pastries.

There was perhaps only one thing that Ashish did not allowed Aniruddha to do. To let Ruchi interfere in his life any more.

He made him realize that just by not coming to the temple 'she has proved that she never loved you'. It was that the first time that Aniruddha agreed to it.

'Love is not the destination of life.' Ashish was seen quoting. Aniruddha never investigated whether it was a stolen dialogue or his own brainchild, all he did was to understand the meaning beneath those words and relate it to his life.

With the period of training coming to an end both concentrated into their reports. Meanwhile their batch mates from other hotels also started returning. Everybody returned and shared their piece of experience.

'The girls from IHM Kolkata were awesome' Kaustav in his very knack of wooing girls started. In minutes the whole area was full with the boys. Sometimes they whispered in each other's ears, sometimes pulled legs or sometimes discussed in the open. They laughed on some and abused in between.

'The private college girl from Delhi was ready for everything with the sous chef for good remarks. And the chef, yes he made full use of his authority.' Ajit showed his anger.

As for me I felt some of these comments were true, others were pickled.

The discussion which initially started with girls in training shifted sharply between hotels and training. 'I could learn a lot about Italian cuisine after working at *La Piazza*' Binayak was quoted as saying. He was talking about products like *Tapenade, Grano Padano, Prosciutto*, etc which Aniruddha has read and seen only in books.

'Aniruddha what did you see? I mean what you did?' he joked on to Aniruddha.

'Just peeled onions and cleaned commodes.' He smiled.

Kaustav felt like peeing on Binayak's face. 'Aniruddha without seeing anything is on a better level, he knows the basics.' Kaustav said but Binayak smiled showing his teeth like an orangutan.

The mob disintegrated in some time leaving behind Ashish and Kaustav with Aniruddha.

Aniruddha was expected to be silent. May be he was hurt by what Binayak intended to say. His past was so tough that these small incidents could do nothing to his smiling curve of lip. 'I missed you,' he said to Kaustav.

It was good to hear this sentence from him; otherwise it

looked as if Ruchi had a copyright on the same if it comes from Aniruddha's heart via his vocal cord.

They were back in the jolly mood. Laughing, chirping they reached Manoj's restaurant. I joined them too, to dig into the favorite aloo parathas which I was missing all these days amidst posh hotel food.

The second year at IHM Bhubaneswar crawled to finish with the announcement of exam dates. The nights were now less comforting as everybody succumbed to do overtime, courtesy the bunking and time-pass throughout the year.

Aniruddha and Kaustav were still bindaas. They left it on to the night before the exams. Aniruddha in particular had a motto- 'NO LATE NIGHT STUDIES'.

Few uneventful days and the exams were over.

The exams gave them a vacation to be back to home. Forty five days or may be a little more than that, everybody was back.

From the very first day of the semester, all the students had Campus Selections in the back of their minds. Al- Qaeda had done their best to make us struggle more for our jobs.

We used to meet regularly in the evening to do a SWOT analysis. Everybody knew their strengths, weakness, opportunities and threats, but practically did nothing to improve. Where communication was a weak link for Ashish, Kaustav was not that much technically strong. For Aniruddha his confidence was drained. May be his love for Ruchi had squeezed out so much of it that though he made the best of *Rogan Josh* in the college, his *josh* was still timid.

And finally the interviews. Kaustav came shouting. 'OCLD (Oberoi's Centre for Learning and Development) interviews at the Trident in just two weeks.' He was gasping as he came running after collecting the info from the placement in charge.

Soon it was made public. Mr. Paul, our placement in charge uttered in his shrill voice as if his vocal chords were lined with grated ginger, 'As you all know, OCLD has the highest standards and we expect you to reach to that level. Last year only a single candidate could make it through to the OCLD. The vacancies are limited but we wish you all a great luck ahead.' Only he knew whether he was motivating us or it was the other way around.

Everybody knew it was tough, but to give it a try was no harm. We were grouped into bundles of ten for our preliminary round- The Group Discussion. Aniruddha was still tensed as if he still had it in his mind that if he makes it to OCLD, he would get his lost love.

Kaustav started the discussion on 'Chef- a cook or administrator'. 'Until a Chef is a good cook, whom will he administrate? What say Mr. Aniruddha?' Kaustav gave him a chance.

Aniruddha could not reply. All because he was scared. He started after some hiccups, but his body language betrayed him. He was out, right there in the first round.

Just for your reference, I made it to the final round.

Series of placement interviews took place. With each interview, the number of unemployed was being reduced, but Aniruddha was still in the list getting smaller. Some was too good for him and for some, he was too good. He made it to the finals of Taj, but could not clear the final. With him was Ashish, repeating the scene of the Industrial Training, but this time they have some dedication.

Barely a fortnight was left for college to end. Everybody who had a job were planning and anticipating about the same and all without it were tensed to find one out. The exams had little importance after looking into the past records of the previous third year students.

The protocol suggested that the campus would bid farewell to us which will be an alumni function as well.

All were supposed to choose their own way and thus had moist eyes amidst scintillations surrounding. Designer suits for few and sarees for others. Though no cocktails were served, mockails were sufficient to spill out whatever we had deep beneath our souls for anybody, of course good, if not the best. All the emotions of the world had a temporary address today at IHM, Bhubaneswar.

Plays, speeches and music were on but in the whole group Kaustav was missing. Soon he came shouting 'Baba...Baba...' and then gasped before saying anything.

'Call in this number, immediately.' He said to Aniruddha. Aniruddha was perplexed, and why Aniruddha only, everybody was.

Was anything serious....in the family....back at home.....or something out of the blue?

'Give me your cell phone' Aniruddha asked.

Call from a PCO. It's very important and you may not hear it right in this huge noise. They ran out of the campus followed by Ashish.

'But what is the matter? Why don't you tell me?' he asked irritated, tensed at the same time.

'This is Ruchi's Number.' He gave some time to Aniruddha to settle down after that thunder and again said- 'Siddhartha called me up few minutes back and said that he was with Ruchi at Dhanbad and she wants to speak to you.'

Though Aniruddha was dumb, the case was not different with Kaustav and Ashish. Kaustav was out of his wits and Ashish, grimaced enough. 'Why...why would she interfere with his life like this when .....' He recalled how tough it was for him to take Aniruddha out of that vicious circle.

'Do you love her Aniruddha? Do you trust her? Now? After all that happened in the last 4-5 years? Kaustav asked, against his nature. He was serious. The situation made him so.

Aniruddha was still dumb. His silence gave the answer. 'Aniruddha, call her.' Ordered Kaustav and winked. *'Baba sala pucca Devdas hai.'* He smiled at Ashish.

Thankfully the PCO was vacant, courtesy the college event.

As Kaustav dialed the number, Aniruddha felt nervous. It was same when they were dating and today also when they don't. The reason, however has transformed.

Kautav handed the red slim receiver to Aniruddha with the first ring and both focused on him. His hands were shievering, I still don't know why?

'Hello' said Aniruddha in a very meek voice.

'Hello.....and how are you? It's been long na, since we have spoken! But I agree it was entirely my fault. I did not share my e-mail id with you. But far from that, you know what, I am selected for IIM. We can make it big now. We will be friends as earlier.' Ruchi spoke in the most enthusiastic way possible.

Aniruddha was awestruck. His mind was in whirlpool of thoughts caught between Ruchi's words and their probable meaning. He was unsure whether he has got Ruchi back in his life or not. He could pronounce nothing more than a 'Congrats.'

'Aniruddha forgot all his worries and surrendered himself to the magical tranquility. He took a deep breath, enough oxygen to start a new life.

'Bye.' Said Ruchi. 'But don't call me. I will be at home for the next one month. I will call you on your friend's number when possible.'

'Bye.' said Aniruddha, smiled and looked on to heaven. He probably re-capitulated his conversations with the sadhu at the Ram Mandir. The other two danced, elated.....as if their biggest wish was fulfilled.

We had hardly few days left in the campus. Some had few days break before joining their jobs; others had to do it instantly. For Aniruddha, he had none. But his level of energy was at all time high. May be the call itself, or few messages or the e-card he received from Ruchi.

MUMBAI

*F*inally, with some desires and consent from Ruchi perhaps, he decided to go to Mumbai. Seeing everybody off to their respective destinations, after a three long years journey was tough, but that's the way life is.

Aniruddha along with Ashish boarded the S3 compartment of Konark express. His old suitcase still accompanied him, and the train journey, as always exciting for him; however it was more thrilling this time. First, he was up to Mumbai. Second, Ashish was with him. Third, He got Ruchi back.

'So, what are the plans ahead?' Aniruddha asked, being very much dependant on Ashish.

'We will start with the ITC Hotels. They have opened a new one called GRAND CENTRAL in Mumbai and the hiring is about to begin. We might have a very good scope.' Ashish was very positive.

'*Kshitiz Bhaiya* will come at station to receive us. We will stay with them for the initial couple of days.' Ashish added.

Ashish's acquaintance with our seniors had provided them a big respite. Otherwise, they were in these new city, carrying ten thousand rupees each, few suitcases and hold alls, certificates, little bit of talent and a big dream to chase.

For Aniruddha the chase was more as he knew he had only couple of years to get into a good position. Ruchi was also about to join her college in a week's time, making her able to speak to him regularly.

All he was thinking while passing barren fields across the rails was to marry Ruchi. Yes but that did not deter him from enjoying the train *masti*. He was relieved than what he was few months back. He obviously got down the train at Secunderabad railway station to get Biryani from 'ALFA'. They enjoyed their first Vada Pav , of which they had so much heard of at Pune Jn.

The train was scheduled to reach Dadar by 4.00 am. They too had to disembark there. Keeping their luggage ready they slept on their upper berths. All of a sudden around 4.00 am or so, there was huge noise in and around the door, waking Ashish up.

'Bombay aa gaya kya?' He asked somebody.

'Haan' was the reply.

Spontaneously he shrugged Aniruddha, waking him up and bringing him down. 'Come fast. We have reached' He commanded. 'We don't need to go to the last station.' He added.

The duo came out of the train. Happy, to put their first step in Mumbai. They felt relaxed, smiled at each other and gazing at the accelerating train soon the blue colour vanished in front of their eyes and what remained was the yellow and black board announcing the station name. 'THANE Jn.'

'Shit, this is not Dadar, its Thane!' exclaimed Aniruddha. 'We are in a soup. Now, we don't know how far Mumbai is.' He completed.

'But why did the men in train tell you that we reached Bombay?' Ashish questioned, bothered with the situation.

They knew nothing about Thane except the fact what Aniruddha recollected. 'The first diesel engine travelled in India between Bombay VT and Thane Jn. for a distance of 50 Kilometers approx.'

'That means we are not far as we don't need to go till VT also. Soon, a VT bound Kerela Express entered the same platform.

'Will this train go to Dadar?' Aniruddha asked somebody and confirmed with another. They got into the train and soon reached Dadar.

It was 5 in the morning. The station wasn't crowded, and but not vacant either. Ashish called Kshitiz Bhaiya from a PCO. None of them had a cell phone.

'Aniruddha could make out after the discussion that they are supposed to go still ahead to Andheri.' Kshitiz Bhaiya perhaps guided Ashish the way out.

With little effort and help from the public they reached Andheri. The name sounded familiar, more so because it was a common address for most of the production houses of televisions and serials, including Khana Khazana.

Kshitiz Bhaiya received them at Andheri railway station, and took them to his flat where 4 other seniors were staying. Though the welcome was warm and hospitality was immense, still Aniruddha if not Ashish felt little hesitant. He was not that close with these seniors in college.

But the brotherhood extended and the motivation provided along with food and shelter, brought Aniruddha back to normalcy.

Mumbai did not appear like the Mumbai they had expected. Not even like Delhi what Aniruddha had seen few years back. Mumbai had chaotic, dingy streets and lanes. But Bombay was good. An evening stroll ended up in a visit to the Gateway of India and some other sights of Mumbai, but the real picture evolved only with the hunt for job. He started liking it.

Morning started with an early bath and soon they left for walk-in interviews. They bumped themselves into the local trains between Andheri and Churchgate and in other routes as well. The huge mass of people pushed them in and out of train. The only place on earth, perhaps, where your competitors are your supporters.

For Ashish, the triumph appeared soon for he was selected as a Hotel Operation Trainee in the F&B Service department by the ITC. Aniruddha was still in the hunt, he was willing to be a Chef.

'By the way, which cuisine you intend to choose if selected to work on?' Kshitiz bhaiya questioned Aniruddha in the evening while preparing dinner.

'Continental' He replied, as he peeled the potatoes for the curry.

'But in India, Indian and Oriental foods rock. Isn't it?'

'I feel it's just the taste that matter. Let me make some Continental stuff out of the dinner materials tonight.' He suggested.

Kshitiz Bhaiya smiled. 'Okay, carry on.'

In an hour, would be Chawal, Dal, Sabji and Chutney were transformed into nicely plated Steamed Rice with Lentil Soup, Spicy Mashed Potaoes and Tomato Fondue.

Kshitiz Bhaiya, as a chef, appreciated a lot.

The search for job finally ended when he got a call from the Taj, where Kshitiz Bhaiya was working. May be the *'Tomato Fondue'* had something to do with it.

On his way to the interview, he called Ruchi. She had now arrived at her college in Ahmedabad. 'Wish me luck' He said.

'All the best, and don't worry. Everything will be fine.' The words were more motivating and pleasing for the personal life rather than the interview. He started feeling Ruchi even closer.

Sitting amongst a group of seven other contenders, he was wondering how many rounds he had to face. 'Aniruddha Trivedi' the HR assistant announced.

'Yes' said Aniruddha raising his arm.

'Please get inside. He said pointing towards a cabin.'

'May I come in?' Said Aniruddha and peeped inside. Middle aged Chef with strict looks was waiting for him.

'Yes please and sit down.' He said. 'I have seen your resume and I am not quite interested to know more about you. Let's talk cooking.' He added to which Aniruddha shook his head.

'What is the best dish you can make?' Chef questioned in a straight forward manner.

'Boiled Rice' was the reply after a prolonged thought.

Chef smiled. 'Interesting.' He said. Tell me the differences between a Souffle' and a mousse'.........

And he grilled him for forty five minutes with *basting* and *barding* and related technicalities, before he said- 'You are through with me, but there is one more round. You need to cook a three course *table-d-hote menu* . Best of Luck for the same.

'Thank you Chef' Said Aniruddha and walked out.

Happy he was, and he called Ruchi again.' Through with the personal interview. One final trade test left.'

'Good' she replied. 'I am also settling down at my hostel. My classes are from Monday.' she added.

Aniruddha flashed like a bulb in the evening in front of Kshitiz Bhaiya. 'I have cleared the personal interview and now the trade test. He smiled and said 'I Know, I work there.'

Aniruddha did everything right on the trade test to complete his three course continental menu.

Gazpacho

Roulade of Chicken Breast served with Garden Greens and Demi Glaze

Crepe Suzette

And now there he was sitting once again in front of the HR'S desk. His appointment letter was in his hand which designated him as Trainee *Chef de Partie* with an annual CTC of Rs 1,28,000.00/-

Aniruddha heaved a sigh of relief. He knew it was a good platform to be at a respectable position in two years.

For Aniruddha, autumn was about to come in few years. All these years he had been playing around either in the scorching heat of summer, or got drenched in catastrophic rains. He remembered the dreams he has seen with Ruchi, back there in Bokaro.

The PCO's number flashed once gain in Ruchi's mobile phone. 'You know what; I have won the MISS FRESHER award for this year.' She spoke in thrill, without allowing Aniruddha to start. She remembered the PCO number now.

'That's great. I mean amazing. Things are getting better for us now. You know, finally I got the job.' Aniruddha said as he wished to say in past that he had made it to the medicals.

'Congratulations' Said Ruchi.

'To both of us'

'Ya....Actually.

'By the way, I feel like meeting you.' Said Aniruddha.

'Me too. We will plan it in some time.' Replied Ruchi.

And they disconnected the phone. Aniruddha was still holding the receiver, lost in his own world. Perhaps he dreamt of a long hug ahead.

U NEVER KNOW

Two months into the job, Aniruddha had earned few currencies and a lot of praise. He had gifted himself a mobile phone and was in constant touch with whomsoever he wanted.

'So, what's your status on the mission?' asked Kshitiz Bhaiya. He was by then aware of everything about Aniruddha.

'Just don't know how instrumental this job will be, but I am glad that I am doing up to my maximum.' Replied Aniruddha.

And she?

'Both of us are focused on our careers right now, missing each other.

Aniruddha called me, Kaustav, Siddthartha, Jaya and whom not.

Everybody had same questions or rather expectations. 'How is it going with her?'

An innocent smile was the reply each time. Perhaps he was also feeling embarrassed.

A few months passed and Ruchi got deeper into her curriculum. So did Aniruddha in his quest to rise up in his career.

A whole year completed and life was once again molded into a pattern. A late wake up in the rented one room kitchen at Andheri, freshen up, a quick bath and rushing to take the 9.45

local for Churchgate to be well in time for the so called 11-3 and 7-11 Break Shift.

Working at the Zodiac Grill restaurant in the hotel was a matter of respect, but the break shift did not impress him much. Though he tried to utilize the time by sleeping in the staff bunkers and dreaming life with Ruchi, but it was not as pleasant as it sounds.

Stinky socks and the perspiration soaked vest combined with the fart if any was tough to handle.

A stroll around the gateway and few calls to friends and family completed the break. Ruchi was perhaps in both the list, until one day when he called her.

The call was disconnected.

And he called again.

It was again disconnected.

He repeated.

And she received. 'Don't you understand I am busy? For you Aniruddha it's just a petit job, for me it's a matter of lifetime. Moreover, I have a personal life as well.'

'But I got tensed as you did not pick the calls...' and before he could complete, she disconnected.

Aniruddha felt dejected. 'What personal life?' He was amazed. Choked with his own tears, he removed his glasses trying not to cry. 'May be she was not in the best of her moods.' He tried to reconcile himself.

'I LOVE YOU' He messaged her and went to the kitchen for the dinner session, waiting for a beep from his phone showing- 1 new message.

Neither did the Souffle' rise properly that evening, nor the caviar looked appetizing. Someone has rightly said- 'Love is a major ingredient for all the foods, more so if the cook imparts it.'

Series of slip-ups in the order that evening till the show ended at mid-night. Out of the hotel, he walked past beside the Arabian Sea, with the sounds of waves hitting the periphery. The moon light walked across the sea to boost Aniruddha as if nothing has happened. And yes 'nothing has happened' is what he said to himself. The moon, few taxiwallas and may be some night shift hotel staff accompanied him, as he walked the distance up to the Churchgate Station.

Unable to command his emotions, he ended calling her once more. He had never called her so late. The recorded voice of the lady said that she was busy.

One more call and the same result.

And the third said 'It is switched off'.

Back from the Churchgate station, he arrived at the hotel. He slept in the bunkers. The environment did not affect him now. He wanted to cry his heart out, but who would listen. His infinite sets of neurons were again put into fight as before. As of now they were almost used to this.

It was pretty late in night or probably early in the morning his phone beeped. Hurriedly he checked his phone. 'Ashish Calling.' It displayed. It was perhaps first time ever that he was unhappy seeing that name calling him. He was wishing it to be her.

' Haan Bol.' He started.

'You have not reached home, not even informed me.....have you started some business....Renting your ass or what?' Ashish shouted and joked to ease.

'It's not funny.'

'Tell me what happened? Chef fucked your happiness or someone else?'

'Ruchi' ....and he narrated.

'There's nothing to freak about that. It's just like a day when somebody fucks your happiness, nothing seems right. Something similar might have happened with her.' He consoled.

'You both are made for each other.' He added. It was more of a wish than a belief.

'I hope so.' Said Aniruddha and walked to the bathroom to take a steam bath.

The 11-3 shift ended swiftly as the break was full of expectations. Probably the first time in the last 24 hours he regained his positives.

Changing back to his casuals from the Chef's attire, he walked down the lanes of Colaba and dialed her number.

The first went missing and the rest were disconnected until she switched her mobile off.

'Is it over?' He asked to himself, but could not answer. He stood still like an idol in the rowdy lanes, resting his back on a café wall. A hawker was selling roses and everything flashed in front of his eyes in an eastman color print. With the strength left in his heart he took Ruchi's passport size photo out of his wallet and looked at it.

'Why you did it with me? Why again? How many times?' He wanted to ask her all these and many more.

And before he could conclude anything out of these events, his phone flashed once more. Someone was calling him. Some unknown number. He quickly responded with optimism.

'Hello…' He said.

'Is it Aniruddha?' A soft unknown female voice said.

'Yes' He said slowly.

'Hi, this is Sakshi; Ruchi's friend. I called up as I found you calling Ruchi. I feel that you like her and I have heard something similar from her as well. But now days I feel she is not interested in you as she is dating someone else. I thought that maybe I should tell you. Any ways, take care.'

Now the basic instinct of human, Aniruddha was jealous. As long as Ruchi was playing little games of hide and seek in his life, his expectations were positive, but now with the entry of a different person in her life, it was unbearable as never before.

He did not cry. How could he? Burning from inside, the heat had taken all the moisture out of him. Gradually he was turning taut. He moved aside, near the shore. He wished, he would sit there till the dawn, but the waves giggled on him behind the heritage 'Gateway of India'.

Aniruddha returned to the hotel for the evening shift, unhappy. The Sadhu at Ram Mandir seemed to be untrue. With his ambitions depleted, his trembling feet inched towards the staff entrance of his hotel. To his embarrassment, or perhaps guilt of loving a girl who was least bothered about his sentiments, Aniruddha was lost. He mumbled few words as he changed into his Chef Coat. With the toque in his hand, he moved towards the banquet kitchen.

Chef Bansi had assigned him to boil huge quantities of spaghetti. With the water boiling in the tilting pan, he put the pastas into it and drained them as they turned al-dente (just done). All these perhaps in an half hearted effort with his mind pre-occupied with Ruchi.

The water was boiling. Aniruddha tilted the pan to drain the water and he screamed and fell down. His limbs and legs were shivering and the face covered with the froth coming out of his mouth. His teeth were locked with each other.

He actually had an epilepsy attack. The disease had hit him again after a gap. The hot boiling water falling directly on his thighs and legs was unable to spark any senses. The chaos within the whole kitchen was brought to a halt, but no one responded. Everybody behaved like statues for few seconds and Aniruddha getting blanched in the hot boiling water.

By the time he was pulled aside by people around, he was badly burnt. He came to his senses with extreme pain in his body. His head was heavy as well. The hotel car rushed him to the nearby ESIC hospital. The standards of the five star hotels and the ESIC hospital were in sharp contrast. Stray dogs, who were otherwise pet in that hospital were roaming lazily and the even lazier doctors and nurses had nothing more than a half squeezed tube of Burnol for Aniruddha.

Aniruddha was laid in a bench, with the car driver standing near his feet and a colleague breathing out stream of cool air off his mouth into the burn legs. This cooled him a little, but it was very less as far as the pain was concerned and soon he again lost his senses. This time it was the pain that made him unconscious.

The news of this incident spread like fire and soon it reached Ashish. Probably Kshitiz Bhaiya did the needful. In his restaurant, possibly serving some *claret* or *burgundy* (wines) to some distinguished guests, he managed to get rid of his job for the moment and rushed towards the hospital Aniruddha was admitted. The traffic blocking his way and his patience was being continuously screened.

As Ashish reached the hospital, Aniruddha was still unconscious. Though some doctors had started to stare him and study the burn, his condition had surely worsened.

The doctors observed the extent of burn and referred him to some big hospital. Soon Aniruddha was in an ambulance with a compounder and Ashish, heading towards the Lilavati hospital. Perhaps Ashish agreed for whatever these doctors questioned about expenses.

It was again a contrast scene than the last experience. Aniruddha was put into an air conditioned cabin and soon few doctors surrounded him. Though Aniruddha was referred to Dr. Saxena, but due to her absence an intern Doctor came to his rescue. 'Dr. Jyotsna' she was being called as.

She immediately started her diagnosis and noted facts on a sheet clipped on a card-board. Second degree, high pain, unconscious, redness, inflammation and blistering were some terms she wrote on her notes, and soon called Dr. Saxena. She probably gave her some tips and then only Dr. Jyotsna started with some first aid.

Minutes later, a nurse called Ashish inside the cabin. 'Good Morning doctor,' he said at almost quarter to ten in the night.

Dr. Jyotsna looked at him and smiled. 'Please be seated.' She said, pointing towards the cushioned chair. Slightly wheatish complexion, with a nice smile on a cute face and her cordial behavior gave some poise to Ashish as he sat on the chair.

'There is nothing to worry for, but the burn will take some time to heal.' Said the doctor. 'But I need few details about him' she added, pointing towards Aniruddha.

Ashish nodded and came closer.

He detailed the incident as it was told to him, stressing that he was under stress and he fell because of epilepsy.

'And how are you related with the patient.........Aniruddha right?' she questioned.

'We are friends. We live together here at Mumbai.' Ashish wanted to focus on the second line so that the doctor paid enough heed to Aniruddha as he is alone in Mumbai.

'Doctor......' He said and paused. Without knowing what to say ahead, he just stared at Aniruddha. He was still unconscious.

'Don't worry.' She smiled and winked. 'He is my friend as well now onwards, though I have many with this name.' she added to give some composure to Ashish's anxiety.

The doctor inspected Aniruddha once more and guided the nurse for the course of action in the night. 'Good night.' She said to Ashish and left for her chamber.

Sitting beside his head Ashish, caressed his face. ' Aa...s. shish.' He heard, coming out of Aniruddha's mouth. His tongue was dried, eyes struggling to open.

Leaving Aniruddha, he ran out and called the nurse and subsequently the doctor. ' Usko Hosh Aa Gaya.' He shouted.

Though the empty room was crowded now but the silence still persist. The doctor again examined him and injected in him few liquids with scary needles. The nurse tried to inject them on his buttocks but failed as he had scars around. The doctor took over and injected on his arm. All these were probably to minimize the pain. The bottle of saline water was replaced with a new one.

Without much attention to all these proceedings Aniruddha slept. Perhaps the injections had a dose for it as well.

Dr. Jyotsna did not leave this time. Instead she sat beside Ashish and started answering to many of the thousands of questions coming in Ashish's mind.

Ashish: By when do you think Aniruddha will be fine to go back work?

Dr. Jyotsna: Probably three weeks.

Ashish: And how long would he require staying back in Hospital?

Dr. Jyotsna: Probably three weeks.

Ashish: What!!!!

Dr. Jyotsna: Yes, you said you live alone, who will take care. Anyways, we will see to it. But I think working for him in a kitchen is dangerous if he has epilepsy.

Ashish: But it does not happen always.

Dr. Jyotsna: But whenever it will, it can be fatal. Why doesn't he change his career to something relatively safe? Does his family know about this disease?

Ashish: Yes, they do, but they presume that it is cured now. He is taking medicines since long. It never happened in front of his family since he left Dhanbad for his studies.

Dr. Jyotsna: Pardon…what you said…..Dhanbad!!!!!!

Ashish: Yes, both of us are from Dhanbad.

'One minute.' She said and moved towards Aniruddha and smiled. 'Aniruddha………. Trivedi.right?' she confirmed his name.

'Lambu, she said to herself.' Her eyebrows shrunk.

'I never knew we will meet like this.' She said to Ashish. He was dumbstruck.

'Do you know him? I mean how?' Ashish had still many things to ask.

'Yes, he was my batch mate at DAV Public school at Dhanbad.'

It was dawn till they discussed about Aniruddha from their viewpoints.

Dr. Saxena examined Aniruddha in the morning. He administered him few tablets and capsules and was pretty happy with the way Dr. Jyotsna had handled the case. 'He will be fine soon.' He said to Ashish patting his back.

A week into the treatment and Aniruddha had recovered fast. Ashish was always there for him. The twenty one privilege leaves that he had earned to visit his home was depleting, but as always there could be nothing dear to him as Aniruddha.

Dr. Jyotsna was not far behind. She extended her shifts and managed with her staff members to take utmost care of Aniruddha. He was now able to cope up with the pain and could sit and talk few minutes; however had no clues about Jyotsna.

One fine morning, Ashish told Jyotsna- 'let's check whether Aniruddha recognizes you or not.' She nodded in reply.

'Aniruddha, she is the doctor who treated you, not as a doctor only but as if you are her family member.' Ashish introduced the doctor to Aniruddha. He has seen her around but his senses were not under his command all these days.

Aniruddha gave a courtesy smile and said 'Thanks'

'That will not do chef. I need a good treat- A special dinner cooked by you.' Jyotsna replied. It was first ever situation when somebody greeted Aniruddha like that.

'And excuse me; I also need to settle all those unresolved matters pending during school days.' She said to put Aniruddha's mind in a whirlpool.

He gazed at her; his mouth open and he finally smiled. His awestruck face moved towards Ashish and back to Jyotsna to finally utter something. 'Jyotsna right?' He asked.

'No. Dr. Jyotsna.' Replied Ashish. Aniruddha wasn't impressed.

'Whatever.....I will call her Jyotsna only. But what a makeover! The pony tail has given way to nice curls of hair and......' Aniruddha pointed out.

'But you could not make out who I was, until I gave you a hint.' She replied.

'Any ways tell me more...I mean you...medical...when...' Aniruddha wanted to know everything.

'Everything will follow. I am here only.

A couple of weeks more and Aniruddha was discharged from the Hospital. Jyotsna and other doctors strictly advised Aniruddha not to continue working in Kitchen.

It was almost a year in the city for Aniruddha. But the summer was different this time. The life what he dreamt with Ruchi had now collapsed. His career had come to a pause if not halt. Unsure of what has to be done ahead, he was just waiting. He spoke to some of his seniors.

With all the consultations over the weeks, he thought he will not wait long.

'How about joining the F&B Service department' Aniruddha asked Ashish.

'Well', He nodded and said nothing.

'Aren't you confident about me working there?' he asked.

'No, means you will have to start all over again.' Ashish replied.

'But that's a common problem in each case.' He debated.

'And the focus that you have put in Kitchen will be lost.' Ashish added.

'That already has.' He replied quickly.

'And your shaky hands?' Ashish finally came out with his actual worry. A genetically gifted problem was associated with Aniruddha.

'What do I do then?' He shouted, probably at himself.

The hefty lunch of Chicken curry and rice cooked by Ashish, and a quick nap followed by a cup of lemon tea gave him some poise. There was no rush for him in Mumbai. The evening sun drew him out and he went to the nearby shops.

He went to a cyber café. There was chaos around. Pre-medical results were declared on the website. He smiled after a long gap, probably on himself, or on his luck. Students were coming out of the café with mixed expressions where sadness outnumbered the happy faces.

Somehow he managed a Computer and started to check his mails. Quickly he updated his resume at Naukri.com and left.

Returning from the Cyber cafe, he called up home. They did not know anything else than the fact that Aniruddha has resigned from the job. 'Because I was not enjoying the work and the work load was too much.' He was heard quoting it earlier.

He spoke long and hung up. Tears stung his eyes, unable to limit it within the perimeters of the eyelids.

Few hours in the terrace later, he was again busy with his phone. It was Jyotsna this time. She used to call him quite often now. Few boosters for Aniruddha and a friend for Jyotsna in the otherwise vacant city of thronged Mumbai for Jyotsna. Indeed symbiotic it was.

'Wassup?' She started.

'Hmmm…*Desi Murgi Bilayti Chaal*!!!!!' he replied. '*Hum acchhe hain. Tum kaisi ho?*' He added in his intentional Bihari tone of which he was sometimes proud off.

'All is fine. Just finished a hectic week and I am off for tomorrow. How are you planned?' she was enthusiastic in asking that.

'For me it's all the same.' Aniruddha stopped midway. Jyotsna was quick to continue.

'All that you need right now is not a job but a vacation or a refreshment to fight back. Let's meet tomorrow.

It was the same Dadar station where he first landed in Mumbai. Aniruddha moved across the platform meekly in the hope that god will turn things even in his life where everything was disturbed.

Splitting the pandemonium of the station enclave, he took few right angles in the street and soon he was in front of the Siddhivinayak temple. Jyotsna was waiting for him there.

Both of them queued up for the Darshan. Aniruddha was too appalling in his appearance contrary of what he was at the Ram Mandir in Bhubaneswar. Untrimmed moustaches, unshaven beard and hair not combed ....but that's how a Devdas look is. Top of that his career had also gone for a toss. I would not have been surprised if he would skip his clothing.

An hour and thirty minutes in the queue and they finally reached in front of the divine Siddhivinayak. He bowed in front of lord Ganesha but was not allowed to stay there long unlike the Ram mandir. Probably the god there had to cater a huge population here.

'Tell all your wishes in the ear of that mouse.' Said Jyotsna, pointing into the two big silver mice in the temple courtyard.

He queued once again and soon came out with little satisfaction. Probably he felt that his application was acknowledged.

As they came out of the temple, his phone rang.

Yes. It was the acknowledgement from god. It was a call from a famous pizza chain against his candidature in naukri.com

'Okay Sir, I will be there at 11.00 am for the interview.' Aniruddha said happily.

'Good, now prepare for your interview tomorrow.' She replied.

'Yes lets go back home.'

'Look you can't do much. So get rid of the anguish in your mind so that you are fresh for tomorrow.' She said and dragged her towards the taxi. 'Bandstand Bandra', she told to the cabbie and hopped inside. Aniruddha followed.

Positive energy was poured on to him by Jyotsna throughout, as if somebody is coating a pancake with honey.

The setting sun at the Bandstand was the best thing to look at. 'Look, everything happens at the will of the god. These waves, the setting sun, the birds and all these people around..... Whatever they are doing is being controlled by god. And don't worry whatever he does is for good.' Said Jyotsna.

'You speak like a sadhu....oops sadhvi.' Replied Aniruddha.

'Might be, but you do whatever that gives you happiness. The world is not over without Ruchi and working in kitchen.'

She debated. 'Anyways, how do you find that girl with blue dupatta?' She was quick to bring some humor. Aniruddha smiled.

With the sun out of their view, they moved to the nearby café coffee day. The chilled frappé had cooled him from inside, whatever Jyotsna could not.

The next morning was different. Aniruddha felt confidant and happy. He narrated everything he shared with Jyotsna the other day to Ashish.

With all the knowledge he had about Pizzas; he bumped into the Interviewer's cabin.

'Why do you want to join us?' The interviewer had a protocol question.

'Just because I don't have a job and am looking for one.' Aniruddha was as straight forward as ever.

After continuous hits and misses, he was finally awarded the job.' Asstt. Manager Store Operations' the offer letter announced. Salary? Better than the last one.

***

Aniruddha heaved a sigh of relief as Jyotsna knocked in their 1 BHK apartment at Andheri. He came to the door in an instant. Ashish was on the way and all of them had a plan for a great dinner.

'Kya haal hai, Koi Mili?' She asked.

It had been three months that Aniruddha had joined his new job and Jyotsna had constantly asked him about any new girl in his life. But for all those questions, Aniruddha just had stupidly stretched lips.

He did the same again.

With the sip of a thick concoction of milk and tea powder with sugar, she said- 'Look you need a girl. Why don't you find one?'

Aniruddha was a bit surprised today, but he retorted. 'You know na, I was cheated on. I don't want to be cheated again. She even got married. I saw her pictures posted on Orkut.'

'Shameless creature.' Said Ashish, as he entered. 'You still bother to check her on Orkut.' He added.

'It was obvious. She dumped you because she wanted to marry someone else.' Said Jyotsna as she sat cross legged on the Kurl-on mattress placed tidily on the floor.

'Why can't you come out of this sick situation? Now that you are getting into a good job, make a new beginning.' Ashish said while he entered the bathroom, slamming the door hard.

'He is stupid. Jyotsna, you tell me; is it that easy to come out of it particularly, when you love somebody so very much?' Asked Aniruddha, in a very low voice so that Ashish does not hear.

' Hmmm……. Aniruddha, it's too long to be continued in this fashion. What is it? I can't understand. Is it a game of hide and seek, or you are fooling yourself.' Said Jyotsna. Her eyes were wide.

'She will come to me one day.' Aniruddha said, desperate to hear a support. 'She has to love me back. How can she not? He added.

'I wish you could understand love!' Jyotsna said in frustration.

'It's best to be aloof of all these.' Ashish said, as he completed chanting the Hanuman Chalisa. Let's move for dinner.

'Where?' Asked Jyotsna.

'Wherever.' Said Ashish. 'How about *Kaffe Kona* at the Linking Road?' He suggested later.

'Cool, I love the Arrabiata there.' She said.

Aniruddha kept his silence until the lemonades were served to them. Neither did anybody prick him.

'Cheers!!! Said Ashish, lifting the Tom Collins glass, filled till the rim.

Jyotsna blinked a couple of times waiting for Aniruddha to add cheers. He did and Jyotsna followed.

As the first sip ran down the throat, Ashish said, 'Jyotsna, you should ensure that Aniruddha gets out of it. After all you are the main culprit.'

'Did I spoil the relation between Aniruddha and Ruchi?' Jyotsna asked surprisingly.

'No, you started.' Ashish spontaneously said. He gave her a crisp summary of what happened with her photograph few years back, making her amazed.

'Well, in that case I will make it up for him.' She responded after a while.

'How?' Ashish said as the waiter came with Penne Arrabiata, Cheesy Garlic Bread and a Smoked Chicken Pizza in thin crust.

She grinned and said, 'I love …….. Penne Arrabiata.' The pause quite understood.

An MBA, a doctor, an IAS or even an illiterate…….if it is a female, they are the best diplomats.

Leaving few ten rupee notes on the Bill folder as tips, they walked away towards the door to ensure priority service next time they check-in.

The autowalla drove them down the SV Road and they dropped Jyotsna at J B Nagar. 'All the best for tomorrow.' She said as she hopped out of the three-wheeler. The auto drove out releasing smoke.

The next day was a big day for Aniruddha. But as of today, he was impatient. He slept with his jeans on. Even Ashish did not speak a word to him rather than the usual reminder for medicine.

At 2.00 in the night, he woke up and opened his suitcase. Yes, the same one. He segregated few documents in the dark. The only light in the room was a fringe coming from the crescent moon. He stood up to take his wallet from his back pocket and removed a black and white photograph.

Ruchi was smiling in the photograph which had deteriorated with time, similarly like her love for Aniruddha. Aniruddha knew it now. He has been told this earlier as well but today he agreed. He smiled and tore the photograph into tiny pieces, tinier than the card given by Ruchi he once tore, right in the outset of his tale.

Lastly, when he tore the card, he joined them back. He did not want it to do the same this time. Quickly he took them to the Indian style water closet and flushed them out.

'Good....Perfect.' said Ashish with a grin as he switched on the room light. 'But don't do the same with these cards and letters. They will choke the pipeline and will give you more distress in the morning than Ruchi gave you in all these days.' He smiled.

'She loves you man...Go for her!!!' added Ashish. Aniruddha was dazed.

A friend pulling you day and night out of a mirage called love, if pushes you for the same is a real matter of shock. Isn't it?

'I am talking about Jyotsna.' Ashish said.

'You are kidding.' He answered.

'She cares for you. Look into her eyes. You charm her.'

'It's not me. Aniruddha said. It's the Pasta...Penne Arrabiata...

'So you are already jealous of Penne Arrabiata.' Ashish was spontaneous.

They got into their sleepers and walked out of the flat into the highway. A chaiwala, vending tea and coffee late in the night from his cycle at the crossings was the only source of something to munch. With two plastic cups of tea and a packet of Good-day Biscuits they sat on a sponsored cement bench, which is otherwise captured by stray dogs or drunken men.

'You have known her since years. She is your school friend. Consider it.' Ashish re initiated.

'That is it. She is my friend....' Aniruddha protested.

'Even Ruchi was someday a friend of yours'

'Forget it. She is a doctor. What am I?

'You never know.... A Restaurateur can be big!' Anyways you are going to start a new day tomorrow.

Over the next sixty minutes, they debated. 'Have a goal in life and then live.' Said Ashish.

'Even you have started speaking like Sadhu....*Bhosdi K.*' Aniruddha said.

They returned to the chaiwala but he left the place.

'Look, it's all about time. The chaiwala has gone. Don't let Jyotsna go away.' He smiled. Ashish has always been his best buddy.

'Will see' He replied and dozed off.

LAST LEAP

*a*niruddha reached his office fifteen minutes prior to the desired time. A long journey of forty five minutes or so in the overcrowded BEST bus took him to Powai. It was a well furnished office, not so big though. He was seated by the receptionist and was told to wait till the HR Executive joins him.

Posters of Pizzas were around. He wished to have one for the fact that they were looking appetizing and he was out without any breakfast.

'Should I get some tea or Coffee for you sir?' the receptionist swung his attentions from the melting mozzarella towards the caffeinated beverage.

'Anything would do.' said Aniruddha.

The fifteen blank minutes forced Aniruddha to think more beyond the Pizzas. He decided to call home, may be to strengthen the odd lose nerves.

'Good na. You will be a manager now. You have done Hotel Management, so you must be a manager. Also this company of yours is quite popular. Everybody knows it. It comes in TV advertisements. The hotel never featured on any Television.' Though she tried to boost her son's morale, his mother was as naïve as ever.

He was looking for someone else who could understand the importance of this step in his career. He called up Ashish but he didn't pick up.

Instead beeped a SMS 'All the Best'. It was Jyotsna.

The HR executive was all set by then. The joining formalities were completed and he was put as a Manager under Training for the first couple of months.

To start with he was trained in theory regarding the Company Mission, Vision, Rules, Operating Procedures and what not. But the practicals were from the scratch.

He was posted in one of the outlets and was told to report to the outlet Manager. It started with mopping floors, but Aniruddha was quick to climb stairs and soon he was managing an independent outlet.

Over the next six months Aniruddha was totally engrossed in his job. Ruchi almost was flushed out of his brain. Might be Jyostsna was swarming in. Nevertheless he rarely spoke to her. His confidence grew with time and all the damage done by Ruchi was being recovered.

Six months into this job, Aniruddha had done full justice to his role and designation. Contrary to this, his outlet was not performing well. A dip in the top-line and bottom-line of his financial statements were regularly seen.

He was summoned to the corporate office.

The auto rickshaw was moving slow amidst the crowded Andheri-Kurla road but imaginations ran randomly across his mind. Will I be sacked? What next?

For the first time he was sitting in front of Mr. Manoj Sharma, Business Head; after he was interviewed by him. Leaning into his table He asked- 'So what is there that's pulling you down'.

Reasons were plenty but none transformed into the shape of answer. Aniruddha rested himself against the back-rest of the chair.

'See Aniruddha. Take things easy. I have not called you here to punish or yell at you. Your store is one of our non performing stores since long. When I interviewed you, I hoped that you might pump in some life.' He said, making Aniruddha comfortable.

'I am sorry sir that I could not reach to your expectations.' Aniruddha said in a humble tone, bit relieved than what he was few minutes earlier.

He smiled in answer, and put forward a very straight question. 'Okay, tell me what had you done if you had been the owner of this Restaurant?'

Sir, whatever I experienced in the last few months, 'I can see that our Restaurant is located away from the target market. This hits our top-line. The high rentals and food cost is hitting us hard on the operating cost. Most of the staff has lost interest to work there. In a situation like these where a restaurant is incurring losses since last 18 months of its start up, we must be brave enough to shut it down.'

'You seem to be a very bold decision maker' said Mr. Manoj.

'May be, but was that a wrong decision?' he was getting fluent and comfortable with each dialogue.

Mr. Manoj just smiled at his answers or rather his questions.

'That is still a debatable topic. You might use your logic when you own a restaurant.' Manoj said smiling, switching the AC off.

'I wish I own it soon.' Said Aniruddha, adjusting his spectacle.

'So? Get one. Put in your talent and explore.' Said Manoj, making things unexpectedly comfortable for Aniruddha.

It was Aniruddha who smiled this time. His smile had a lot too many queries. 'HOW?????' He thought.

'Do you smoke' Asked Manoj as he picked up his Marlboro Lights and a lighter from his drawer.

'No sir, Thanks.'

'Okay, Do it passively and give me company' He said with yet another smile and walked into the lawn.

The crisp crease in his shirt and trouser was drawing equally importance as his smoke rings. For Aniruddha, his top Boss's closeness to him was difficult to understand. Amazed he looked for motive behind all this.

'Look Aniruddha,' He started but paused for a puff and then continued, 'I have a habit of talking straight. My main reason to call you here is more personal than official.

He stopped for few seconds for another couple of puffs, keeping Aniruddha wondering.

'I want to open a Restaurant but I have certain limitations in the way I want it do. And that's where I want you to pitch in as you are also interested to run an independent restaurant and is surely capable of doing that.' He completed.

It came as a bouncer to Aniruddha with so many open ended questions. The most obvious one was- 'But I don't have money at all to open a restaurant. How can I partner with you?'

'There you are wrong. Ask me about my limitations first. Okay let me tell you, money is not a problem for me. I will put in all that is required.'

'My main concern is that I cannot leave this job paying me 24 lakhs per year for the restaurant. But you can.' He stressed in his last few words pointing his finger towards Aniruddha's chest.

Aniruddha was in a dilemma and was silent, looking everything between heaven and earth. Manoj was smart enough to read his mind.

'Look you have just joined this company, working at a comparatively lower post and not earning that handsome as well. You are young, bachelor, without any responsibilities as such. Take this small risk and grab the opportunity.' Manoj was well prepared to sway Aniruddha.

'But what if doesn't work out'? Asked Aniruddha in a nervous tone.

'Thinking positive is a must to attain something and if things do not happen our way, look for a job.' He answered.

'But..'

'Just think. It will be your menu, your recipe, your processes, your own selected team, your restaurant. You will be big'. Manoj expressed as if he is visualizing all what he said.'

'Can we go for some tea sir? I am getting confused.'

'Sure.' Said Manoj and smiled. He walked with big strides in the building corridor with Aniruddha.

'Sir I really don't understand how will this happen? Do you want me to work with you as a manager? Will you give me salary? What all do I need to do?' Aniruddha put series of questions to him, all that he was bothered with, as he sipped from the cup.

'No. It's very simple. You will be my partner where I will pay your share along with mine and in return you will do my work along with yours.' Manoj described but Aniruddha was looking into some other threads as well.

'How much ownership you will have in the business?' Asked Aniruddha, now looking at it practically. He thanked his professor at IHM for all the little fundas that he had in accounts as of now.

'Once the capital expenses are recovered, we are 50% shareholders.' Manoj put it very spontaneously.

'Sounds good sir, but how will I survive till we recover expenses? Asked Aniruddha.

'Don't Worry. These are petty things. Will be taken care of.' He smiled and winked as Aniruddha complemented.

Aniruddha was still little puzzled about all happening around. He did not even leave the last drops of tea in the cup. Few unstrained granules of tea sticking to his tongue.

'Go, think and let me know. I believe your answer will be positive.' Mr Manoj tried to ease him.

The whole journey back from Office to home was swift.

'When are you reaching?' Aniruddha scream over his cell phone. He wanted to discuss it all with Ashish at the earliest.

'Bas Ek Ghanta Baba. I have left and is on my way' Replied Ashish from the other side.

One hour was a pretty long time for his in this juncture.

He sat crossed legged on the mattress with his chappals on, and scratched his head.

Never in the past was he ever so confused, not even if it was related to Ruchi.

He scrolled down the contacts in his cell phone only to stop at 'J'. 'Should I call her now?' And before he could get any answer from within, his finger pressed the green button.

Jyotsna replied spontaneously with a 'hello.'

'Can you come now? I need to discuss something.' Asked Aniruddha.

'Hmmm....Okay. will be there in sometime.' She replied.

Tea making and surfing channels did not make it to one hour. Aniruddha finally had to resort to the Newspaper lying aside.

'Entrepreneurs of Tomorrow.' An article read. He imagined his picture in that article and started reading.

'Hi. How are you? What happened... all of a sudden you called?' Jyotsna checked in with lot many questions?

'Call Ashish, and check where he reached.' Said Aniruddha in reply and tossed his cell phone.

Ashish disconnected the call after few rings and soon entered. 'What happened? What are you so mad about? 'Oh, Hi. You are here!' He added as he saw Jyotsna.

Ashish might have smelled something fishy but the suspense was ended by Aniruddha with a smile. He looked confident and determined now.

'Well, I was waiting to take suggestion about a decision, but now I have finally decided something.' Said Aniruddha, as if acting in a stage.

'What?' Said both of them in unison and anxiousness.

'I have decided to open a restaurant.' He said.

'Don't just joke. Tell fast. Why were you so anxious and calling me so desperately?' Ashish said.

'I am not kidding.' He said with convincing eyes and narrated the whole chapter with Mr. Manoj.

Things were tough to believe, but tougher to settle on. 'Will it be the right choice?' was running across Ashish and Jyotsna's mind.

Aniruddha however had taken a decision. He picked his phone and dialed Manoj's number.

'I am ready sir. When should I start?' He asked enthusiastically. He was looking passionate and charged as never earlier.

'Cool down dude. Enjoy couple of days and then we will start. It's an uphill task ahead.' Replied Manoj.

The evening ended with some celebration at Kaffe Kona.

A dozen of documents waited to be introduced to Aniruddha on Manoj's centre table. 'Come inside.' He said to Aniruddha in the utmost hospitable manner showing him the couch.

The well lit and elegantly decorated 3 BHK apartment of Manoj was bringing him some unease against the 1 room Kitchen where he stayed.

There was another person in the hall. 'Meet him. He is Mrigank. Chartard Accountant, and my cousin. He is there to help you with all the accounts and compliances.' Introduced Manoj.

'And he is Aniruddha. The guy I told you about... my so-called partner.' He added with regular intervals and smiled.

Mrs. Sharma entered with 3 mugs of coffee and placed them in the same centre table.

'Look, we have already completed with the process of company formation. Its Aaura Hospitality Pvt. Ltd. Mrigank will do the needful to make you a part of the same as per our terms.' Manoj Described sipping the hot Coffee.

'But is it that important?' questioned Aniruddha.

'Yes. Without these, you won't get your licenses, and lease agreements done. These are the basics.' Mrigank spoke for the first time.

'Aniruddha, by the time Mrigank gets these done, I expect you to come up with BRAND name, Concept, Model, Location,

Menu, Vendors, Staff and others. May or may not in that order. But the first thing I need is an expected Cost for everything.'

Aniruddha smiled and shook his head. The task was bigger than expected.

He stood up and moved across the table to reach the rack displaying books and magazines. 'I need few of them for some ideas.' He wished.

'Of course you will and listen take this and carry out a small research on what, when, how and for whom.' He said as he handed him a bundle of five hundred rupee notes.

"In the midst of all these, my career took a sharp turn when I was selected for AIR-INDIA.

With my posting at Mumbai, I bumped into Anhish and Aniruddha.

I had a better understanding of all these developments around in some time.

Soon Jyotsna too was equally friendly."

*

'People will always come back for some Indian cuisine here. It's their cuisine.' I suggested. After long time, I was also a small part of this story again.

'Go for a Chinese restaurant. Indians like it this way' Suggested Ashish.

'But both of these are in plenty and there is nothing new to it. Let's think of something that had never been before.' Aniruddha said and scribbled something on a piece of paper.

TYPE: *Coffee Shop/ Multi cuisine/ Speciality Restaurant*
CUISINE: *Indian/ Thai/ Mexican/ Chinese/ Italian*

Looping the words with his pencil he added 'We can do a speciality restaurant, which can have all cuisines.' His eyes looked delighted as if Archemedes discovered buoyancy.

'But that would mean a multi cuisine restaurant. Isn't it?' Ashish asked in irritation.

'Yes, but how special is that if we do it for only one product. Say......chicken or fish or mutton or may be even Prawn!!'

Everybody including me was wondering at this idea. 'You will get limited customers.' Ashish said.

'May be initially, but with good marketing and a steady product and service, we can gradually add to the count.' Aniruddha looked confident in what he decided as he said this.

'And what will be that product' I asked.

'I guess the chicken sells most and the prawn least. So, people have least idea about prawns, and its cooking. They might be delighted with the array of products that can be made with Prawn.'

'But you are reducing your target market even more. I mean non-veg, then sea food plus the affordability. You know Prawn is expensive.' claimed Ashish.

'May be you are right in your logic. But I feel the concept would work. Let's settle on it.' Aniruddha said.

Everybody smiled back in affirmation.

Aniruddha called Manoj and updated him with the proceedings.

'As you wish, man. I have full faith in you.' He replied.

*

Location was the next agenda. Confused with built up area, carpet area, lease rentals and security deposit, he turned to Manoj for guidelines. Manoj guided him with processes and the general market rates across the city.

Meetings with estate agents and landlords at various locations gave him some idea now. He settled for a site at Juhu Tara Road. 'Twenty five hundreds square feet at ground level on the Juhu Tara, just opposite to J W Marriot .' He updated Manoj over phone.

'And the Rentals?' asked Manoj.

'Three lacs per month were quoted.' He said slowly moving away from the landlord.

'Let me check tomorrow if its possible.' He replied.

Aniruddha along with Manoj, Mrigank and the agent drove down to Juhu for finalization of the site.

'Looks good.' Said Manoj as he walked across the room and coming out.

'This site has a very good potential sir. We had a restaurant here earlier and it did too good.' The landlord claimed in his sales talk.

'Why did they shut it down then?' Asked Manoj.

'Some partnership issues sir. You Know na…..'

'Okay, whatever.' Manoj cut him short. May be he did not want any tension in Aniruddha's mind which those words could fetch.

'The rental looks little on the higher side. Say, what can be done?' Asked Manoj.

'You will do great business here. You will have no problems.' The parsi landlord said in his bawa accent.

'If it is so let's keep it this way. The rentals will be 2.5 lacs per month or 18% of Net Sales, whichever is higher.'

The landlord remained silent for couple of minutes and said Okay. Perhaps he was calculating how much the earlier restaurant used to sale.

Their caravan halted next in a coffee shop to discuss future course of action.

'Why don't you speak to Chander for the fit-outs?' asked Manoj.

'Who Chander?'

'The guy who does it for our company. He is good at his work and might give us a good deal.' Manoj suggested between the sips of his cappuccino.

Aniruddha saved the Business card of Chander in his mobile phone, sent by Manoj.

'It will involve a set of processes. I need to check the site and discuss the way you want it to be done. Do you have somebody for the interior designing and creating kitchen layout?' Said Chander in his first conversation with Aniruddha.

'Oh, that's a lengthy phenomenon.' Aniruddha Thought.

'No, no one for interior designing, but I might plan the kitchen' Replied Aniruddha.

'Okay, then I will get Jasmine, my interior designer along with me tomorrow.' Said Chander, as they ended the tele call.

Lease registration followed the next day. The registrar's office at BKC looked as chaotic as ever but for Aniruddha, first time in this course, he was practically feeling the ownership as she signed the documents on behalf of Aaura Hospitality.

Mrigank had done the needful earlier to make Aniruddha a part of the Aaura Hospitality.

Couple of follow-ups and finally Chander arrived with Jasmine. A forty plus man and an early twenties lady or rather a girl. Some measurements in feet and inches and then all settled down.

'You need to tell us about your layout in the kitchen and we will come out with a 3D image.' He insisted.

'So the menu has to be decided before the fit outs' Aniruddha thought.

'Okay you start with the basic plastering and I will get you the layout.' Aniruddha suggested.

Mr. Manoj was having a submarine view of all these proceedings. He evolved wherever necessary to make things simpler for Aniruddha or to save cost as in case of Chander. He had sanctioned a lot of his tenders in the past for this very occasion.

Designing Menu was entirely Aniruddha's Job. He called Kshitiz Bhaiya and many others for this and gradually composed one.

Staffing was a continuous process. Few were suggested by Mr. Manoj itself from his other company and others were sourced via medium like Kshitiz bhaiya and other known faces around.

Things were moving as per plan until one day, when Aniruddha woke up late. With nobody around, he checked his mobile to find 12 missed calls. He preferred to freshen up first without calling.

At around 12, completing all his other works, he moved to his cell phone. The number of missed calls rose to 15. He never knew that he had kept the phone in silent mode.

He decided to call back.

'Hello, who is this? I mean I got few calls from this number but failed to receive.' Asked Aniruddha

'Is it Aniruddha Trivedi?' came the reply.

It took less than a second's time for Aniruddha to understand that it was Ruchi. He was astonished.

'Ruchi.' He replied instantaneously but with a hesitation.

'OH, you still remember me.' She asked.

'Of course yes, over all those years…..may be you forgot everything.' Aniruddha replied intending some pun. 'So what made you to call all of a sudden' he added.

'Yes I will tell you everything. Actually I felt very bad about what I did to you. I could not sleep the whole night. And so I called Jaya and took your number.' She spoke with pauses between words.

'Oh! Anyways, how is life? I heard you got married and settled in Kolkata.' Aniruddha tried to cool things off.

'Yes. Rightly heard.' She spoke softly.

'Where are you working now and tell me about your husband?'

'I work at ITC as a marketing manager, handling Fiama Brand. Aniruddha, can I say Sorry to you. I know I have lost that right as well. I am Sorry, Please forgive me.' She said changing the subject. There was a paradigm shift in her tone. Emotions come easily to women. Resonance of her sob was clearly audible.

'Please, please don't do that. What is your fault? Actually it was me who was running behind the mirage. You never loved me only.'

'No, it's entirely my mistake. I had been selfish in taking all these decisions. First I dumped you and then I married a guy against Papa's wish.' She replied.

'So what? Forget it. How is Kroorsingh? Aniruddha smiled as he said so.

'He is no more' She replied after a silence. He could not bear my decision; I know how difficult it had been for you to handle it.'

Her statement brought a total stillness in the atmosphere around both ends of the network.

'I am paying for all my deeds.' She added and started crying.

Aniruddha's resistance to melt with her dialogues started giving up. He felt like to reach her and fill her in her arms, so that he can absorb her pain. 'I am there na, don't worry. I will handle now. You know I am opening a restaurant.'

'I opted for copper when Gold was in my hand. Forgive me Aniruddha.' She said as she sobbed without paying any attention to the restaurant part.

'Anyways, I will have to go now. This is my contact number but don't call. I will call when I get time.' She said and disconnected.

The conversation left Aniruddha with too many open ended questions, but the first impulse was not to share this with anybody, even Ashish.

Trials were conducted for the menu, recipes were created, interior was designed, and furniture, upholsteries and equipments were being purchased. Among all, there was a shift in his mood. He was often seen lost in his world.

Few days ahead of the start of the restaurant, Aniruddha was again seen with Ashish and Jyotsna.

'Couple of days and the restaurant will start operating. I am feeling anxious. Don't know how the response will be. Aniruddha said.

'Baba you had never been so worried about career.' protested Ashish.

'It's not about career, but.....' He left it in-complete.

'Don't worry, all your dreams will be fine' Jyotsna tried to lift him.

'Baba, get married. You need a life partner now.' Ashish said smilingly and moved out for his hotel duty leaving everybody smiling

'Can we go out for some coffee?' Jyotsna suggested, after a bit of silence.

Aniruddha nodded to agree.

A lazy walk across few gullies, they reached Café Coffee day at the J B Nagar circle. Both lost in their thoughts even as they sat across the 2 feet circular table.

Aniruddha gazing everything around but looking nothing and Jyotsna wondered what to say.

'What should I get for you sir?' A waitress broke the silence, perhaps thinking that they are here just to kill time.

'A cappuccino for me, and a frappe' for the lady.' Aniruddha said and smiled.

'Oh wow! How did you know that I want Frappe'?' Asked Jyotsna surprisingly.

Aniruddha smiled. 'It's long now....Right?' Asked Aniruddha.

'What?'

'That I ......know you' He replied with a pause.

'But does that enables you to know all about me?' She questioned.

'Perhaps it does.'

'Aniruddha, Can I ask you a question?'

'Sure'

'Do you love me?' Jyotsna was sharp and bold this time.

Aniruddha was shocked. It came to him at a wrong time. May be this question, if asked to him couple of weeks earlier, he would have simply answered positively, but now after Ruchi's call it was tough.

Trying to camouflage his fret, he smiled. 'You know my worries. Let me settle down a bit.' He lied to Jyotsna.

The ice cream in the frappe' gave some cool to Jyotsna. She had told what she wanted to. But the hot froth of the cappuccino added to Aniruddha's anxiousness.

It was long that the two set of neurons in his skull were divided and shouted slogans.

'Anything else Ma'am,' the waitress arrived again trying some suggestive selling.

'Thanks, Please get the cheque.' Replied Jyotsna with a formal smile.

'You know, I have spoken to mummy about you. They are happy and they liked your photograph as well.' She said as they walked back from the café.

Aniruddha visualized Ruchi's mother, her pakoda, cold milk and calling her 'Beta'. Walking with Jyotsna, he remembered all the moments that he shared with Ruchi.

As they reached home, Aniruddha surrendered to the mattress. His cell-phone rang with a vibration. Jyotsna picked it.

'XYZ calling' it displayed.

'Who is it?' She asked amazed.

'The interior designing girl.' He said, quite hesitantly as he took the phone. 'I don't remember her name.' He added to disguise her and received the call.

'Hello'

'Kaise Ho?' It was Ruchi.

'Can I call you in 5 minutes?' He replied and disconnected without letting her answer. 'Maybe I need to leave. See you later.' He said to Jyotsna.

He dialed Ruchi within minutes. 'Haan bolo. Sorry I was with this interior designer of the restaurant.' He lied with the same excuse, but to a different person.'

'Oh ho! Dealing with women now days. Anyways, how is she? *Koi chakkar to nahi chala rahe ho na?*' She tried to pull his legs.

Ruchi sounded relieved and casual today unlike the last day.

'Please don't. I am sick of it now. But tell me one thing, if I marry or say I have a relation, will it hurt you? Aniruddha asked.

'Hmmm, of course a little bit. We were a couple some day.' She said & smiled sarcastically, may be on herself.

'But you are married now. You have a loving husband, I hope?' Aniruddha replied.

' Yes he does, but not the way he used to when we were dating. I mean he does not have time for me now.' She said slowly.

' Can we still be in touch? I guess you understand what I mean.'

'I miss you Aniruddha, in my life.' She added. 'All these days I was trying to compile strength to say this to you.' Her voice showing waves of emotions.

'What do you want from me? Tell me directly.' Aniruddha said.

'Meet me ......please.' Replied Ruchi.

'Let me see.' He said and they disconnected.

The restaurant was to open in couple of days. There were few snags yet to be sorted. So the days for Aniruddha were awfully busy. Hardly he could come home or speak to Ashish or Jyotsna. Not even with Ruchi in that case.

Finally, the day arrived. There was a huge crowd of invited guest, most of them unknown to Aniruddha. His eyes were successful in finding Ashish, Jyotsna and me. Thankfully my flight dates did not clashed with the event.

Mr. Manoj held the Coconut and later handed it over to Aniruddha, so that he can smash it in the restaurant and with it an auspicious start takes place. 'Aniruddha is the main energy behind this' He quoted.

Aniruddha was being introduced to the different guests as his cell phone rang. 'XYZ Calling.' It displayed.

'Haan Bolo, thoda busy hoon.' said Aniruddha.

'I am in Mumbai. I had to come urgently for an audit at ITC Marataha Sheraton. Waiting for you. I will leave tomorrow early morning. I am texting my room number.' She said and disconnected.

No excuse seemed strong enough for Aniruddha to get out of that event. He looked restless.

Unaware of the entire cyclone that had erupted in Aniruddha's mind, Jyotsna walked down to her. For the first time she was clad in a saree and was looking beautiful.

'I am very happy today. You have put a firm step towards your goal today, and I have full faith that one day it will be very big. And listen.....I LOVE YOU. She whispered in his ear the last three words as she stood on her toes. Out in the dark, their eyes met and the lips followed.

Aniruddha realized that Jyotsna was constantly hearing the unsaid proposals of love from him. 'I love you too' He said.

He took his cell phone out and scrolled his contacts. 'XYZ' He selected and pressed the green button.

He flashed the screen to Jyotsna as the rings were going. 'It's Ruchi.' He stated. Jyotsna was shocked.

'Hello.' Said Ruchi.

'Ruchi, Sorry I can't meet you.'

'But why?'

'All of a sudden I remembered the pain I suffered when you trailed out. I cannot give the same pain to somebody else. That somebody who lifted me when there was no one. All the best for your life ahead.' He said and disconnected.

'XYZ Calling' The phone flashed again but Aniruddha disconnected. He kissed Jyotsna's forehead instead.

'The number to which you have dialed is busy.' Ruchi heard.

Aniruddha's phone beeped in a while. It was a SMS from Ruchi. 'You are really gold. I was foolish this time. Let me take birth again and I will chase you right from the maternity ward. Miss u.☹-Ruchi.'

'☺' He replied.

'What is happening here? You both are out for so long, away from the event?' I and Ashish came walking along the lane.

'Nothing much, just sorting a suitable dates for our wedding.' Aniruddha Said and handed over the phone to us to check the inbox.

'And you two start preparations. You have to do all arrangements from my side. I don't have a brother. You know na.' She said and both of us hugged Aniruddha.

Few more messages were shared across at that moment. Aniruddha was unaware of them.

'Thank you' appeared in my phone. Same was with Ashish. It was from Jyotsna.

We smiled in unison and forwarded the same to a number. It was Ruchi's.